The Serpent Myths of Ancient Egypt

W. R. Cooper

With Notes and Remarks by
Dr. S. Birch, M. Renouf, M. Lenormant, S. M. Drach, Esq.,
and other Egyptologers

Ibis Press
An Imprint of Nicolas-Hays, Inc.
Berwick, Maine

Published in 2005 by
Ibis Press, an imprint of
Nicolas-Hays, Inc.
P. O. Box 1126
Berwick, ME 03901-1126
www.nicolashays.com

Distributed to the trade by
Red Wheel/Weiser, LLC
P. O. Box 612
York Beach, ME 03910-0612
www.redwheelweiser.com

Library of Congress Cataloging-in-Publication Data

Cooper, W. R. (William Ricketts), 1843–1878.
The serpent myths of ancient Egypt / William Ricketts Cooper.
p. cm. -- (The Ibis western mystery tradition series)
Includes bibliographical references
ISBN 0-89254-139-3 (trade pbk.)
1. Mythology, Egyptian. 2. Serpents--Mythology--Egypt.
3. Serpents--Mythology. 4. Dead--Religious aspects. I. Title. II. Series

BL2450.S39C66 2005
299'.31212--dc22

2004056855

BJ
Printed in the United States of America

10	09	08	07	06	05
6	5	4	3	2	1

Cover design by Kathryn Sky-Peck.
The paper used in this publication meets the minimum requirements of the American National Standard for Information Sciences—Permanence of Paper for Printed Library Materials Z39.48–1992 (R1997).

CONTENTS

LIST OF ILLUSTRATIONS

THE

Serpent Myths of Ancient Egypt.

BEING

A COMPARATIVE HISTORY OF THESE MYTHS

COMPILED FROM

THE "RITUAL OF THE DEAD," EGYPTIAN INSCRIPTIONS, PAPYRI, AND MONUMENTS IN THE BRITISH AND CONTINENTAL MUSEUMS.

BY W. R. COOPER, F.R.S.L.,

HON. SEC. SOC. BIB. ARCHÆOLOGY.

With Notes and Remarks by DR. S. BIRCH, M. RENOUF, M. LENORMANT, S. M. DRACH, ESQ., *and other Egyptologers.*

Being a Paper read before the Victoria Institute,
or, Philosophical Society of Great Britain, 8, Adelphi Terrace, Strand.
(*With the Discussion.*)

THE WHOLE ILLUSTRATED WITH 129 ENGRAVINGS.

Shrine of the great deity Amun-Ra, with the goddesses Mersokar and Eileithya in the form of snakes on either side of the door. Above are the solar disk and the usual cornice of everliving uræi. (Leyden Museum.)

OBSERVATIONS ON THE SERPENT MYTHS OF ANCIENT EGYPT. Illustrated with Explanatory Figures from Egyptian Monuments and Ancient Gems. By* W. R. COOPER, Esq., F.R.S.L., *Secretary of the Society of Biblical Archæology.*

WHILE much has been done for the elucidation of the Ophiolatry of India, Greece, and Rome by many most able scholars, yet the serpent myths of Egypt,—the oldest, most abundant, and best preserved of them all, have been but little attended to since the time of Champollion and Wilkinson. On the Continent it is true that MM. Pierret, Brugsch, and Lenormant† have published a few isolated papers upon parts of the legends of hieroglyphy, but these have never been translated into English, and even the originals are but little known. This is both a subject of regret and of surprise, for no one who considers the very early connection between Egypt and Israel in Biblical times can fail to have noticed that there were many allusions and restrictions in the ceremonial laws of the latter nation, which only by a reference to the customs of their contemporary neighbours could be duly understood. While the Romans doubted, and the Greeks ridiculed, their gods, the nobler and more primitive Egyptians loved, and were supposed to be beloved, by them. The profane and the impure divinities of the Grecian Olympus, the debaucheries of Silenus and of Pan, the fraudulent Mercury, and the unchaste Venus, find no counterpart in the Egyptian Pantheon. Not till the irruption of the semi-greek Psammetici does Theban worship become obscene, and Theban sculpture gratuitously indecent; and it may be safely asserted, without fear of contradiction, that there is, morally and scientifically, more to disgust in the *Odes* of Horace or *The Days and Weeks* of Hesiod, than in the whole vast range of ancient Egyptian literature.

---

* Those aware of some of the tendencies of modern thought will recognize the value of this paper. Since it was read the author has kindly taken the opportunity of adding such new matter as the most recent investigations on the subject afford, in order that it might be as complete a statement of the serpent myths of ancient Egypt as could be at present published. The engravings have been carefully done on the graphotype process by Mr. John Allen.—ED.

† Mostly in the *Revue Archéologique*, of Paris, and the *Zeitschrift für Ægyptische Sprache*, of Berlin. England as yet possesses no journal wholly devoted to exegetical archæology.

2. The danger of Egyptian theology was not in its innate impurity, but its extremely speculative character, its endless subtleties and misunderstood symbolisms, its fetish amulets, and degrading animal idolatry. In these it was, to a great extent, imitated by the Jews, whom, despite the precautions of the divine lawgiver, it corrupted, while by associating with the visible agencies of good and evil the ideas of invisible and supernatural power, the hieroglyphers, as more or less all symbolists eventually do, obscured the antitypes they intended to typify, and overloaded their imperfectly significant faith by a still less significant system of representation. These errors the pride and subtlety of the hierarchy permitted the common orders to fall into by the division of their dogmatic teaching into an exoteric, and esoteric, meaning,—one for the people and another for themselves,—and then, after a time, avarice and statecraft usurping the place of principle, the bulk of the Egyptians were left to follow their own interpretations of their symbolic statuary, while the secret beauty of the Theoretic faith was reserved for the hierophants alone.

3. Foremost among all the natural objects first associated as representatives, and then as hypostases, of the Deity, were the sun and the heavenly bodies; the sun as Chefer- and Horus-Ra (fig. 1), the moon as Isis, the heavens as Neith; and upon earth

Fig. 1. Horus-Ra, wearing the solar disk and uræus. (Arundale.)

the benevolent and fertilizing Nile as the deity Hapimou, or a form of Khem, father of the land of Egypt. The sanctification of beasts, birds, and reptiles followed—some for their beauty, others for their utility; then a spirit of fear led on the way to the propitiation of destructive agencies and injurious animals —the storm, the east wind, the lightning, in the first class, and the hippopotamus, the crocodile, and the SERPENT, in the other,—till, in the end, after centuries of superstition and decadence, the adoration, vocative and precative, of this latter reptile spread throughout the whole of the Egyptian mythology, and the serpent lay enshrined in the temples of the oldest and most beneficent divinities.

4. From the very earliest period to which our researches are enabled to extend, there is written and monumental evidence that out of three kinds of serpents, known in Egypt and represented on the monuments, *two* were the objects of a peculiar veneration and of an almost universal worship. Unlike the adoration of Seb (fig. 2), the crocodile deity of Ombos and

Fig. 2. The deity Sebek wearing the Teshr or great plume of Osiris. (Bunsen.)

Tentyra,* and the batrochocephalan deity, Pthah, the frog-headed fire-god of Memphis in the Delta, the reverence paid to the snake was not merely local or even limited to one period of history, but it prevailed alike in every district of the Pharian empire, and has left its indelible impress upon the architecture and the archæology of both Upper and Lower Egypt.

5. The three serpents peculiar then to Egypt and North Africa appear to have been: 1. The Naja, or Cobra di Capello, the

Fig. 3. The Sacred Uræus or Basilisk. (Sar. Oimen.)

spectacle-snake of the Portuguese and the Uræus† (fig. 3) and basilisk of the Greeks; a venomous and magnificent reptile, with

---

* Champollion (le Jeune), *Panthéon Égyptien.*

† Uræus, Gr. = Ouro = arau, in hieroglyphics, the letters composing the determinative of king.

prominent eyes, ringed skin, and inflated breast. From its dangerous beauty, and in consequence of ancient tradition asserting it to have been spontaneously produced by the rays of the sun,*

Fig. 4. The solar disk encircled by an uræus wearing the Pschent.

this creature was universally assumed as the emblem of divine and sacro-regal sovereignty.† 2. The Asp, or Cerastes (fig. 5),

Fig. 5. The Cerastes. (Bonomi, *Hieroglyphics.*)

a small and deadly kind of viper, possibly the cockatrice of Holy Writ,‡ remarkable for its short thick body, and blunt and flattened head, crested with scaly horns. 3. A large and unidentified species of coluber, of great strength and hideous longitude.

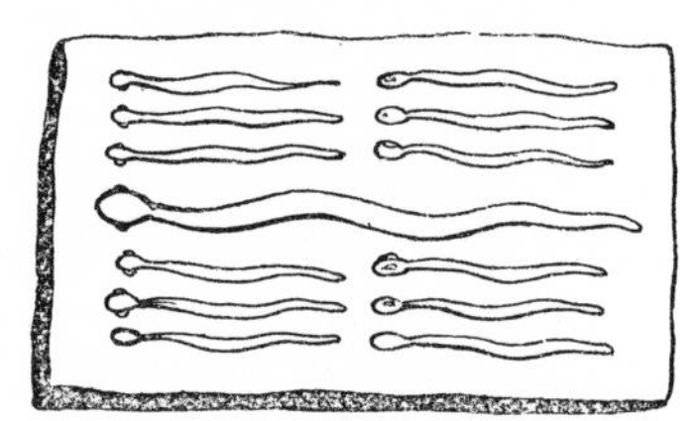

Fig. 6. Limestone tablet in the British Museum, possibly representing the generation of the months.

This last was, even from the earliest ages, associated as the representative of spiritual, and occasionally physical evil, and

---

* Hence the reptile is termed, on an ancient papyrus, "Soul of the body of Ra."

† The King or Pharaoh is hieroglyphically represented by a basilisk (uræus) encircling the solar orb alone, as on the great gates of El-Luxor. (Fig. 4.)

Deane, an unsafe authority, asserts that death by the sting of an uræus was supposed to insure an immortal life to the victim ; hence the peculiar fitness of the death of Cleopatra.

‡ There is a curious block at the British Museum, representing one large viper (distinguished from those commonly drawn by an extremely large head) between twelve smaller ones. The reptile is wrought in soft stone, of ancient Egyptian work, and is unintelligible as to the mythos represented, there being no hieroglyphics. (Fig. 6.)

was named Hof, Rehof, or Apophis (fig. 7), "the *destroyer*, the *enemy of the gods*,* and the *devourer* of the souls of men." That such a creature once inhabited the Libyan desert, we have the

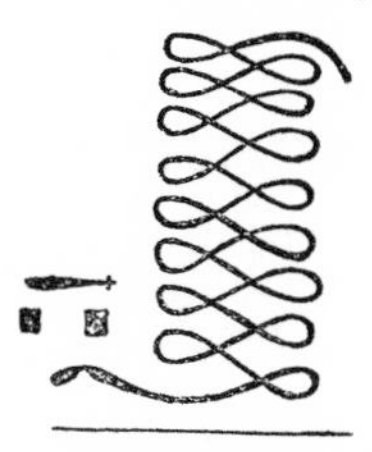

Fig. 7. Apophis, *the destroyer*. The hieroglyphics above his head compose the letters of his name, A—P—P.

testimony both of Hanno the Carthaginian† and Lucan the Roman;‡ and if it is now no longer an inhabitant of that region, it is probably owing to the advance of civilization having driven it further south.

6. With one or other of these snakes all the ideographic theology of Egypt is involved. Does the king desire to

Fig. 8. Thothmes III. wearing the sacred crown of Osiris; beneath it, and above the claft or plaited head-dress, is fixed the jewelled uræus.

declare his divine authority, he assumes the sacred asp of Amun-Ra (fig. 8), and wears the basilisk upon his crown. The

* From Hof or Hf is derived the Coptic name of a snake to this day.

† See *Periplus*, Cory's translation.

‡ First of those plagues the drowsy asp appeared, (Cerastes.)
Then first her crest and swelling neck she reared;
A larger drop of black congealing blood
Distinguished her amidst the deadly brood;
Of all the serpent race are none so fell,
None with so many deaths such plenteous venoms swell. . . . .
Her scaly fold th' Hæmarrhoïs unbends, (Apophis ?)

priests of the Temple of Ra at Heliopolis, and the priestesses of Isis at Alexandria,* carried serpents in their hands or in Cane-

Fig. 9. The basket of the Eleusinian Canephoræ, containing a serpent, from whence the basket of Jupiter Serapis was derived. From a Greek coin. (Sharpe.)

phoræ on their heads (fig. 9) to declare their divine ordination (fig. 10). Hence also, the secret adyta, or sacristies of the divini-

Fig. 10. Egyptian priestess carrying the uræus. From a Ptolemaic slab engraved in Bartoli's *Admiranda*.

ties, and the sculptured arks, with the massive shrines, great

---

> And her vast length along the sand extends ;
> Where'er she wounds, from every part the blood
> Gushes resistless in a crimson flood. . . . .
> The Basilisk, with dreadful hissings heard, (Uræus.)
> And from afar by every serpent feared,
> To distance drives the vulgar, and remains
> The lonely monarch of the desert plains. . . . .
> Lucan, *Pharsalia*, lib. ix. 1200-30, Rowe's Translation.

* Sometimes the Pschent, or Royal crown, was decorated by a cresting of pendent uræi similar to the usual ornamentation of a shrine. See Lepsius, Abth. iii. Bl. 284.

sacred triads, were crested with a cornice of jewelled snakes (fig. 11). As the emblem of divine goodness, the crowned Uræus, resting upon a staff, was one of the most usual of the

Fig. 11. Upper portion of snake-crested cornice from intercolumnar slabs. (Philæ.)

Egyptian standards, and the serpent upon a pole, which Moses, by divine direction, upheld to the Israelites in the wilderness (fig. 12),* has been supposed to have been either

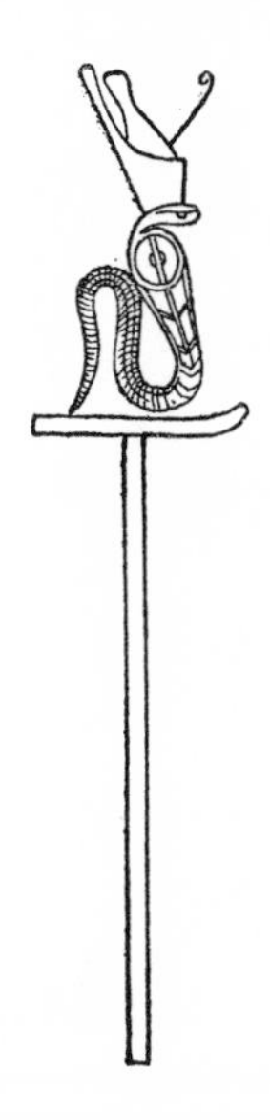

Fig. 12. An Egyptian standard, bearing a bronze figure of the goddess Ranno. (Sharpe.)

an adaptation, or imitation, of the well-known pagan symbol.† Again, when once the Uræus had been associated with the idea of divinity, the Theban priests, rightly desiring to ascribe the gift of life and the power of healing to the Deity

---

* Numbers xxi. 9. † Sharpe, *Bible Texts*, p. 47.

alone, significantly enough twined the serpent around the trident of Jupiter Ammon (fig. 13), and the staff of Thoth,

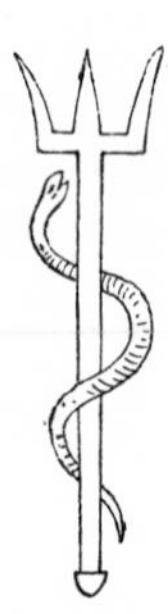

Fig. 13. Trident and serpent of Jupiter Ammon. From a gem. (Maffei.)

or Hermes Trismegistus (fig. 14),* the author of medicine, to imply the source from which that subordinate demigod's virtues

Fig. 14. Staff of Hermes; on the top is the mystic hawk of Horus-Ra, and the solar uræus. (Wilkinson.)

were derived.† From this, in the later periods of her history,

---

* Wilkinson, *Ancient Egyptians*, vol. v. p. 12, plate 46; and vol. iv. p. 183.

† The older Italian antiquaries, whose treatises are as comprehensive in detail, as they are excellent in composition, have written much of this and cognate mythological analogies; as, for example, Cartari, Vicenzo, *Le Imagini dei Dei de gli Antichi*, 1581; Orlandi, Orazio, *Osservazioni: il Serpente di Bronzo*, 1773; Agostini, Lionardo, *Le Gemme Antiche*, 1657. All these are in the library of the Soane Museum, the curator of which affords every facility for their inspection.

Egypt remitted to Greece, along with the so-called forty-six hermetic treatises, the traditional caduceus, or serpent sceptre

Fig. 15. The Caduceus or serpent-staff of Mercury.

of Cyllenius (fig. 15) and Æsculapius (fig. 16),* and by a sub-

Fig. 16. Staff or club of Æsculapius, the god of medicine. (From Maffei.)

sequent transformation of the same deities into a feminine

Fig. 17. The serpent and bowl of the goddess Hygeia.

form, the snake and bowl of Hygeia (fig. 17), the goddess of

---

* On the side of the rock grotto of Trophonios were sculptured images of Trophonios and Herkyna with serpent-twined staves.—Raol Rochette, *Monumenti inediti*, pp. 21, 22.

health.* Following out the same symbolic teaching, to imply the swiftness and extent of the divine attributes, the serpent

Fig. 18. The serpent and dish of the goddess Maut, the great mother.

of good is often invested with wings; not that such creatures ever existed, but to identify the active and passive properties of the divine essence in *one* impersonation.† Instances also occur, as on the sarcophagus in the Soane Museum,‡ where four

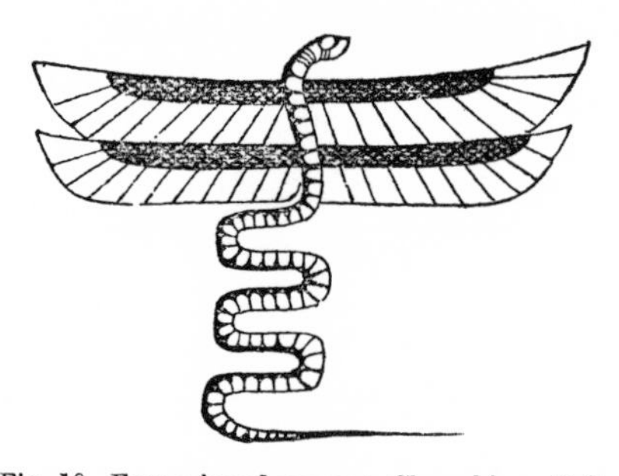

Fig. 19. Four-winged serpent, Chnuphis or Bait.

wings are attached to the divine reptile (fig. 19), that "the four corners of the earth," a completely Egyptian mode of expression, might be represented as being embraced by and sheltered by the Supreme Providence, while in another instance the solar disk is crested with four serpents (fig. 20), the Uræi of goodness, embodying the same metaphorical allusion.

---

* *See* Maffei, Alessandro, *Gemme Antiche figurate*, 1707, plates 55 and 57. The serpent and bowl are doubtless derived from the hieroglyphical characters for Maut, the mother goddess, these being a serpent upon a shallow bowl, which the Greeks, not reading as the hieroglyphical signs for "Lady Mother," modified into mere ornamental attributes.

† Such serpents occur on the sarcophagi of Pepar, XXX. Dyn., in the British Museum, and papyri of Petuk Hans, Hesi Hem-Kebi, XXI. Dyn., and Amen-Shau, XXVI. Dyn.

‡ That of Oimeneptheh I.

Snakes guarded the gates of the eternal region; and snakes were worshipped while living, in the temple of Khonso at

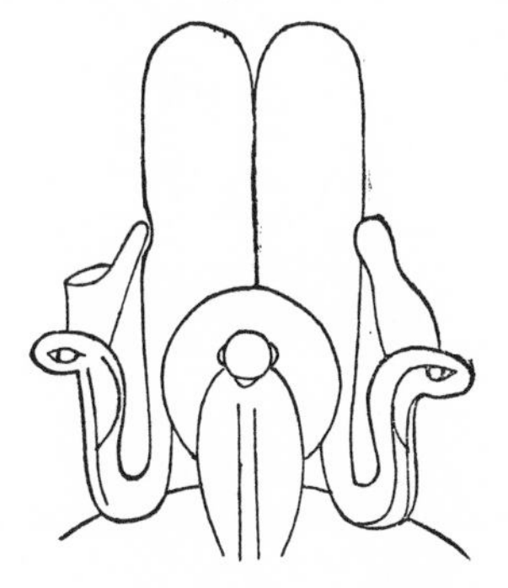

Fig. 20. Plume of Amun-Ra, and solar disk, with four uræi. (Leyden Museum.)

Napata, and mummied when dead in the temple of Kneph

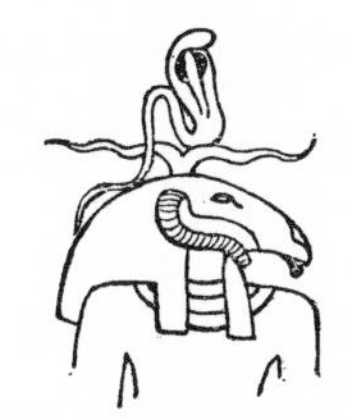

Fig. 21. Head of the ram-headed god Chnum, the spiritual generator, bearing the feminine uræus of Ranno.

or Chnouphis, the spirit or soul (fig. 21) of the world. The

Fig. 22. The symbolic winged serpent of the goddess Mersokar, or Melsokar, wearing the crowns of the upper and lower kingdoms. (Wilkinson.)

guardian genii of Upper and Lower Egypt, Melsokar (fig. 22) and Eilethya (fig. 23),* were honoured under the guise of uræi;

---

* Wilkinson, *Ancient Egyptians*, vol. v. plate 52.

and the avenging Cabereii (fig. 24),* or torturers of the wicked

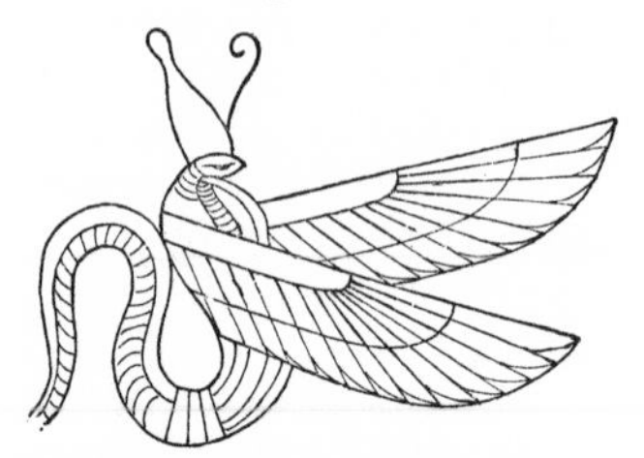

Fig. 23. The symbolic winged serpent of the goddess Eileithya, wearing the crown of the lower kingdom.

in the Egyptian purgatory, inflicted the fellest punishment upon the condemned, by scourging them with whips of living

Fig. 24. The avenging Cabereii, the tormentors of the dead. At the left hand is the Pylon or entrance to hell, guarded by two Cynocephali, the emblematic monkeys of Truth and Justice. (Sharpe.)

snakes, or thrusting them, in company with ferocious vipers,

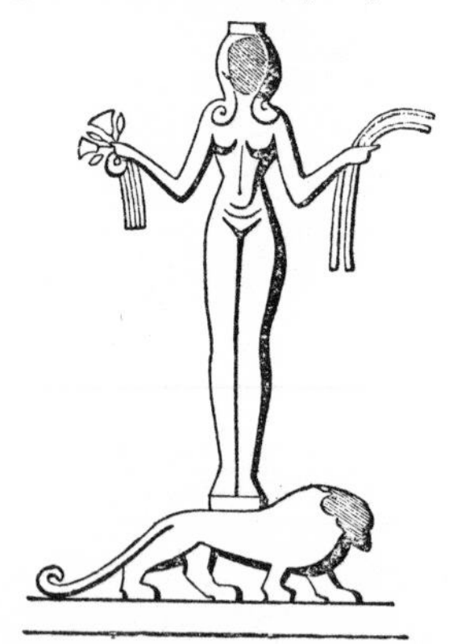

Fig. 25. The goddess Chiun, Venus. From a stelė in the British Museum. (Sharpe.)

into a lake or tank of fire.† The goddess Remphan (fig. 25)

---

* Cabereii, from קבר. Children of Pthah Typhon and his hideous consort Thoeris, the source of the Hellene Eumenides.

† A common representation, which occurs on the outside of several wooden sarcophagi in the British Museum, as No. 38, Upper Egyptian room.

and the younger Horus, to declare their power over life and death, hold snakes in one hand and flowers in the other, offering the symbols of beauty and health to the Egyptians, and threatening the Syrians on the left hand with the envenomed creatures of death.* The Greeks, who, two thousand years later, introduced all these theories into their own mythology, and interpreted the sacred figures of the Egyptians by their own less esoteric cultus, have, through the mistakes of their philosophers, greatly obscured the real symbolism of the ophiolatry of Egypt; and those who would unravel the mysteries of Alexandrian and Theban faith, must begin by disregarding the Olympian Pantheon, and forgetting the perversions of Roman ignorance and Plinian supercilious incredulity.

7. Further, be it remembered, the Egyptian reverence, both in fear and love, of the serpent, was contemporaneous with the lives of the oldest Biblical patriarchs; and to one who is unable or *unwilling* to accept the sacred chronicles and the antiquity of their earliest chapters, it is exceedingly difficult to

Fig. 26. Krishna entangled in the folds of the great serpent Caliya, who is biting his heel; the incarnate deity is waiting for divine assistance from Indra to enable him to overcome the enemy.

account for the prevalence of a serpent myth, not only in Egypt, but in Assyria, Etruria, and Hindustan; † still more difficult is it for such a one to explain the extraordinarily

* Sharpe, *Egyptian Monuments in the British Museum*, p. 70.

† As in the myths of Ramayana and Krishna, and the serpent Caliya. For an exhaustive treatise on Indian ophiolatry, *see* Fergusson's *Tree and Serpent Worship*.

close analogies existing between the very words in which the serpent is described, and the acts in which he is represented as officiating, and those titles and deeds by which the

Fig. 27.* Krishna triumphant over Caliya; with both his hands the deity grips the folds of the hated monster, and crushes its head beneath his feet. (Conf. Gen. iii. 15.)

ancient serpent is painfully familiar to us all in the Mosaic record. A Greco-Egyptian writer of the Ptolemaic period, Horapollo,† does, indeed, assign *a* motive for the superstition; and his language is sufficiently curious to excuse our quoting it accordingly; and here is also the best place wherein to interpolate a few other extracts whose novelty will at least excuse their introduction, though it will be obvious that, from a purely philosophical point of view, the explanation they afford of the serpent-worship of Egypt is unsatisfactory in the extreme.

"When they would represent the universe they delineate a serpent with variegated scales, devouring its own tail; by the scales intimating the stars in the universe. The animal is also extremely heavy, as is the earth, and extremely slippery, like the water; moreover it every year puts off its old age with its skin, as in the universe the annual period effects a corresponding change, and becomes renovated. And the making use of its own

---

* This and the preceeding figure are from drawings supplied by William Simpson, Esq.

† Horapollo, lib. i. cap. ii.

body for food implies that all things whatsoever that are generated by Divine Providence in the world undergo a corruption into it again."*

Fig. 28. The Orphic egg, symbolizing inert matter vivified by the demiurge. (Bryant.)†

This relates to the coluber or serpent called Bait, "soul of the world," alone. According to Champollion, the emblem of

Fig. 29. The serpent Chnuphis. From a Gnostic gem. (Montfaucon.) The name inside the circle is that of the Archangel Michael.

the Creative power of the Deity (fig. 29) under the form of the god Chnuphis (fig. 30), a deity identified with Jehovah Sabaw

Fig. 30. The deity Chnuphis, as a double-headed serpent. (Champollion, *Panthéon Egyptien.*)

(ΙΑΩ ΣΑΒΑΩ)‡ (fig. 31) by the Gnostic heretics of the second century.§

---

* Hence the well-known symbol of a serpent entwined round an egg, used by the Orphic mystics to signify matter vivified by spirit.

† For further details of the great Egyptian Orphic myth which evolved creation out of the cosmic egg, which breaking, the upper half became heaven and the lower earth, see Creuzer's *Symbolik*, ii. 224, and iv. 83–5.

‡ צְבָאוֹת (Tsebaoth), "Lord of Hosts."—S. Drach.

§ See Montfaucon, art. "Gnostiques"; *Abraxas*, tom. ii. part 2.

"When they would represent eternity differently, they delineate a serpent with its tail covered by the rest of its body, and they place golden figures of it round the gods.* The Egyptians say that eternity is represented by this

Fig. 31. The symbolic serpent of the deity IAΩ. (Drawn from memory.)

animal because of the three existing species of serpents; the others are mortal, but this alone is immortal, and because it destroys any other animal by merely breathing upon it, even without biting. And hence, as it appears to have the power of life and death, they place it upon the heads of the gods."†

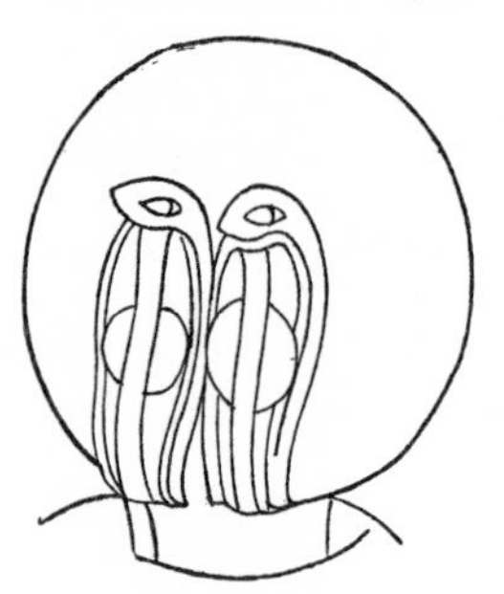

Fig. 32. Solar disk and double uræi. (Leemans.)

This evidently refers to the uræus only, who is frequently represented as guarding the sacred cypress groves of the Amenti (Sheol) by breathing out fire to destroy any invading or unjustified soul ‡ (fig. 33). Hence arose the origin of the

---

* On the front of the head-dresses peculiar to divinities and kings.

† Horapollo, lib. i. cap. i. A curious example of the manner in which a symbol is exaggerated when its significance is misunderstood or forgotten, is afforded by a Romano- or Greco-Egyptian statue of a king wearing the great crown of Amun-Ra, the supreme divinity, with *two* uræi instead of one, on the solar disk; ridiculously intended by the sculptor as a *double* compliment to the monarch.—See *Musée de Leide*, part i. plate 1.

‡ Uræus = אור light— burning furnace.—S. Drach.

Grecian myth of the Hesperidean garden and the *fire-breathing* dragons which guarded it (fig. 34). With respect to the uræus,

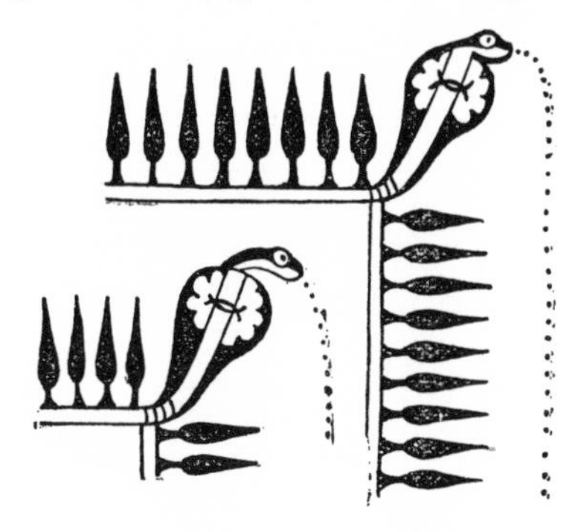

Fig. 33. The corners of Paradise guarded by fire-breathing uræi; further on, but not shown in the plate, are the bodies of the just awaiting in the cypress shades their ultimate revivification. (Sar. Oimen.)

one circumstance deserves notice; it is always represented in the feminine form, and is used as a symbol of fecundity. Hence

Fig. 34. The serpent guarding the apple-tree of the Hesperides. From a Greek vase in the British Museum. (Sharpe.)

all the goddesses of Egypt were adorned with, and represented by, uræi; and not unfrequently the snake is alone figured, with the name of the goddess written in hieroglyphics above (fig. 35). This is notably the case in the tablets from the Belmore collection in the British Museum (see *infrà*, §11, first moiety), and on the sarcophagus of Hapimen, a great functionary of the nineteenth dynasty, and on that of Oimenepthah I., a monarch of the same period. (Fig. 36.)

"To represent the mouth they depict a serpent, because the serpent is powerful in no other of its members except the mouth alone." *

Fig. 35. Jewel in bronze, representing the serpent of goodness, or the goddess Ranno, Greco-Egyptian period. (From the original in the Hay collection.) Exact size.

This latter assertion is not borne out by the hieroglyphics, where the serpent uræus† is simply the phonetic of the letter *g*, and the asp, or coluber, of the letter *f*, or a sound analo-

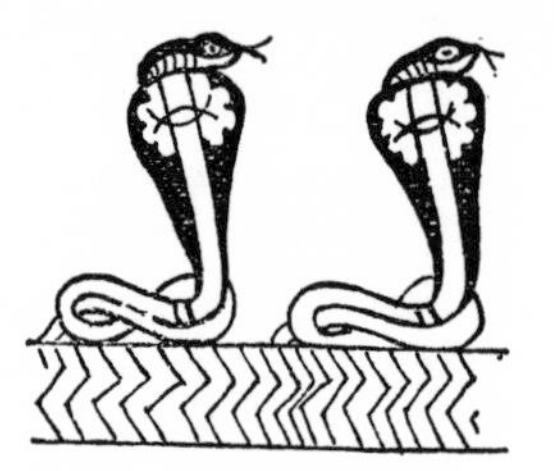

Fig. 36. The goddesses of Heaven as uræi resting by the side of the river of Amenti. (Sar. Oimen.)

gous to the Greek ϕ alone. Possibly it was an error for the name of another snake, Ru, which is the determinative ideograph for mouth.‡ This identification of Pharaoh with the serpent of goodness§ gives a wonderful significance to the bitter apostrophe of the Jewish prophet, who from the river of Chebar, foreseeing the final subjection of the Egyptian empire by the Chaldeans, terms the sovereign of Thebes "the great

---

* Horapollo, lib. i. cap. 45. † S. Drach. ‡ Bunsen, vol. i. p. 545, note.

§ The first king of Abyssinia is traditionally said to have been a serpent. Is this a misunderstood myth derived also from Egypt, whose kings, under the nineteenth dynasty, invaded, if they did not conquer, Abyssinia?

serpent in the waters," as it were denouncing *him* as the serpent Apophis, the enemy and destroyer of his country by his fierce opposition to that god, by whose right hand he, like Apophis, should be overthrown. "Son of man," says the divine afflatus to Ezekiel, "set thy face against Pharaoh, king of Egypt, and prophesy against him, and against all Egypt. Speak, and say, Thus saith the Lord God: Behold, I am against thee, Pharaoh, king of Egypt, the great dragon that lieth in the midst of his rivers, which hath said, My river is mine own, and I have made it for myself. . . . . I will have thee thrown into the wilderness . . . thou shalt fall upon the open fields, and all the inhabitants of Egypt shall know that I am the Lord."—Ezek. xxix. 3—6. Cf. also Isaiah li. 9, and xxvii. 1, where the same reference to the Apophic myth runs throughout. (Fig. 37.)

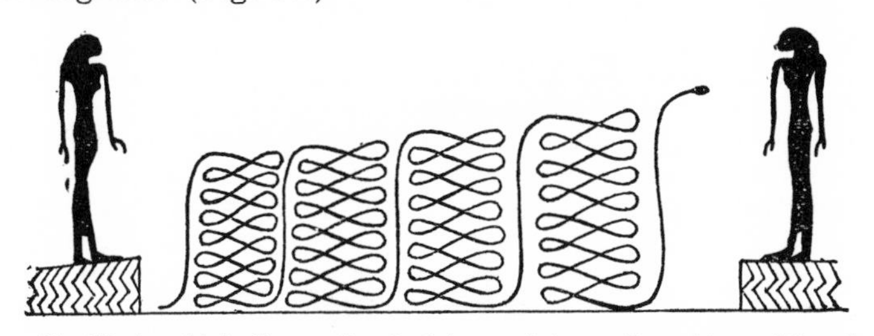

Fig. 37. Apophis in the mystic celestial ocean between the goddesses Isis and Nepthys. (Sar. Oimen.)

8. The uræus is also the ideograph of the word "immortal"; whence the phrase, "the living years of the uræus," as applied to the immortality of the king. (Fig. 38.)

Fig. 38. A Greek coin, representing Ptolemy with the attributes of the Grecian Herakles, and the sacred snakes of the Egyptian Amun Ra. (Sharpe, Lee collection.)

"The asp is worshipped on account of a certain resemblance between it and the operations of the Divine Power, and being in no fear of old age, and moving with great facility, though it does not seem to enjoy the proper organs for motion, it is looked upon as a proper symbol of the stars." *

* Plutarch, *De Iside et Osiride*, § 74.

"In the vicinity of Thebes there are also sacred serpents not at all troublesome to men; they are very small, but have two horns on the top of the head. When they die, they are buried in the temple of Jupiter, to whom they are said to belong." *

This corresponds in some degree to a statement by the famous Principal of the Medical College at Cairo, M. Clot Bey, who asserts † that the uræus, or cobra, is *not* poisonous. Unfortunately the passage from Herodotus implies not the Naja, or Nasha, but the Cerastes, or two-horned viper. The temple of Jupiter is of course that of the god Chefer-Ra, who held a position in some respects analogous to that of Jupiter with the Romans or Zeus among the Greeks.

Cite we yet a further passage, and this time it shall be one from the Great Ritual of the Dead itself. It is the apostrophe to the serpent Bata in "Heaven, where the sun is." (Fig. 39.)

Fig. 39. The serpent Sati, or Bata, on the High Hill of Heaven. (Ritual, cap. cxlix.)

"Say, thou who hast gone, O serpent of millions of years, millions of years in length, in the quarter of the region of the great winds, the pool of millions of years; all the other gods return to all places, stretching to where is the road belonging to him? (*i. e.* who can measure the length of his infinity of years). Millions of years are following to him. The road is of fire, they whirl in fire behind him." (Celestial, not infernal, fire is here to be understood.) ‡

This symbolic creature may be the serpent alluded to by Job, when, in special reference to the works of God in the heavens, he declares, By his spirit he garnished the heavens. His head wounded the crooked (cowardly§) serpent.—Job xxvi. 13. (Figs. 40, 41.)

---

* Herodotus, *Euterpe*, 74.

† Bonomi, *Catalogue of Antiquites, Hartwell House*, p. 22, No. 171.

‡ Chap. cxxxi.

§ Sharpe's translation. נחש ברח Query, "gliding or barred serpent."—S. Drach.

From a misconception or mistranslation of this chapter, it is probable that Horapollo derived his confused account of the

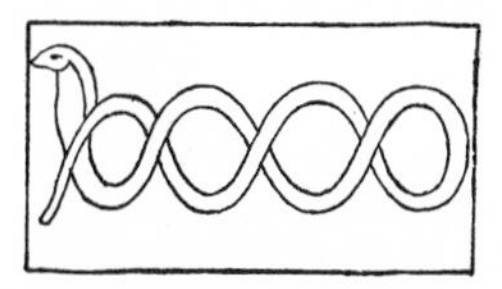

Fig. 40. The constellation Hydra. From the Zodiac of Denderah. Romano-Egyptian period. (Denon.)

serpent myths. Between the Egyptians and the Greeks there was little in common, and the priests purposely misled their Grecian querists, whom indeed they designated and treated as children.*

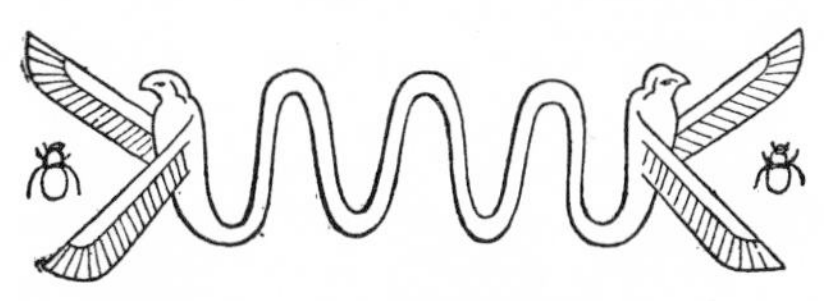

Fig. 41. The same constellation. From the Zodiac of Esné. A little earlier period. (Denon.)

9. As, in the order of Providence, good always precedes evil, we will so far digress from the main purport of this paper, the Myth of Apophis, "the Destroyer," as to dwell for a few paragraphs upon the uræus of immortal divinity, and the Egyptian goddesses symbolized by it. (Fig. 42.)

Fig. 42. The goddess Pasht, or Buto, holding in one hand the Cucufa staff and in the other a feminine uræus. (Sar. Oimen.)

10. The feminine deities were more numerous, and their character and offices were less distinctive than the male divinities. Each and all of them are written hieroglyphically by an uræus alone, sometimes with the ordinary proper name affixed;

* The reply of the Egyptian priest to Solon the Athenian is almost proverbial :—" You Greeks are children."

sometimes with the epithets "living, sparkling, shining, or immortal" (fig. 43); and sometimes, and far more frequently

Fig. 43. One of a series of goddesses adoring Amun Ra, and holding stars as offerings. (Sar. Oimen.)

also, with a mystical compound name, the exact significance of which is not capable of literal interpretation. Often as the feminine spiritual principle, the goddess, as a serpent, twines

Fig. 44. The god Khonso in a shrine; at his feet is the serpent Ranno. (Sar. Oimen.)

round, reclines beneath, or over-canopies one of the greater male divinities (fig. 44),* or with rising crest and inflated

Fig. 45. The god Knuphis, or Chnum, the spirit, in a shrine on the boat of the sun, canopied by the goddess Ranno, who is also represented as facing him inside the shrine. (Sar. Oimen,)

---

* Belmore Collection, plate 18. See also triple mummy-case of Aero Ai, plate 1,—" Num in the sacred barge protected and canopied by Renno or Isis."

hood, protects her protégé with her terrible fangs (fig. 45). The generative power of the solar beams is always typified

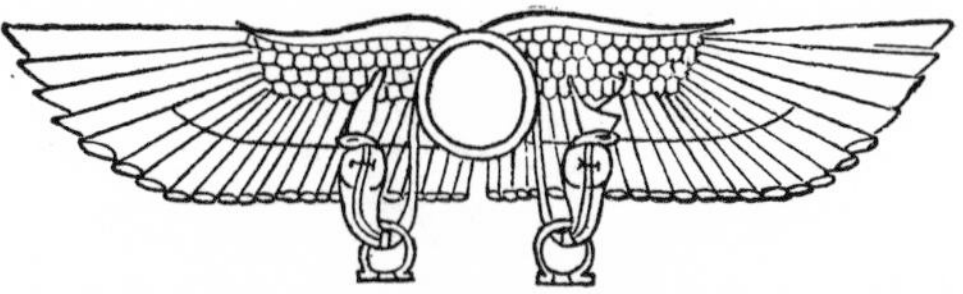

Fig. 46. The winged sun of Thebes. From the great Pylons at El Luxor. (Bonomi.) In this instance the signet of authority is suspended by the serpents in lieu of the usual Tau cross.

by pendent uræi (fig. 46),* which latter have generally the

Fig. 47. The bowl and snake of the goddess Mersokar; beneath is the lily of the upper country. (Wilkinson.)

crowns of Upper and Lower Egypt, representing the goddesses Melsokar (fig. 47) and Eileithya (fig. 48) respectively.†

Fig. 48. The bowl and snake of the goddess Eileithya; beneath is the papyrus of the lower kingdom. (Wilkinson.)

Often a goddess, incarnated in a serpent, rests in a shrine or sits upon a throne to receive the worship of her votary.‡

---

* Wilkinson, *Ancient Egyptians*, vol. i. p. 239, second series.

† *Ancient Egyptians*, vol. v. p. 45.

‡ As in an unique example of the Ptolemaic period in the British Museum, which represents a quadrangular shrine, at the door of which a sitting uræus is sculptured. The cornice is terminated by a pyramidion, and the whole is executed in soft limestone. A nearly, but not quite, similar shrine, is figured in *Musée de Leide*, vol. i. plate 35.

Fruit, bread, flowers, and incense are the gifts most usually presented, human beings and animals, never.* The goddesses

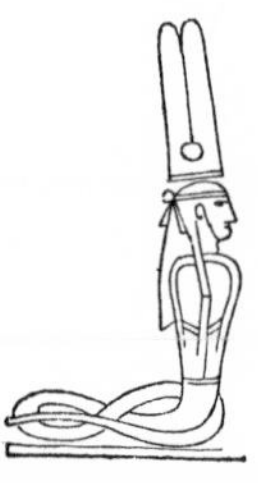

Fig. 49. The sacred uræus of goodness, or the goddess Ranno, wearing the symbolica crown of Amun-Ra. (Sharpe.)

whose cultus has left the most positive traces of its extent, are Melsokar or Mersokcar, the patron of Lower Egypt; Renno

Fig. 50. Shrine, with the sacred uræus. (From memory.)

(fig. 49),† the mother of gestation, and goddess of harvest; and Urhuk, one of the doorkeepers of Sheol or Amenti. Of all

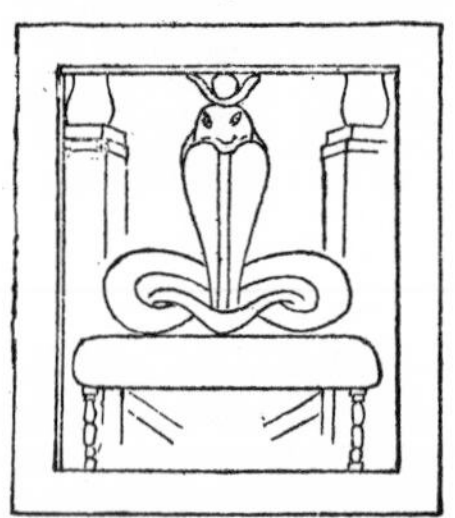

Fig. 51. Shrine, with the sacred uræus. On either side are columns bearing a vase of oil and honey for the food of the reptile. (Leemans.)

these statements, the incised and painted tablets and papyri in the British Museum afford ample evidence; and some of these,

---

* Contrary in this respect to the serpent "Fire face." See *infrà*, fig. 100.

† Curiously enough, the Hebrew word for green vegetation, רענן (Cant. i. 15) strongly resembles that of this goddess. May the word have an Egyptian origin?

and notably so those in the Belmore collection, we will now proceed to describe.

11. On four of these monuments the adoration of one, who, in addition to her other offices, was the patron deity of nurses, women, and children, the goddess Ranno, is represented. In each case the offerings are precisely similar, and consist of flowers, fruit, and cakes. In No. 56, which is unfortunately broken, a Nubian gentleman,* kneeling on one knee, presents the divinity with lotus-flowers and

Fig. 52. Sepulchral tablet in the Belmore collection, representing the worship of the goddess Ranno. (British Museum.)

ornamental leaves, and offers for her acceptance a kind of *wave offering*. † Ranno (fig. 52) is drawn as crawling on the ground before the suppliant; and the serpent's scaly crest is sur-

Fig. 53. Sepulchral tablet as above. (Same collection.)

mounted by a placid human head,‡ adorned with a splendid askh or collar.§ In fig. 53 || the same subject is again re-

* Belmore Collection, plate 8.

† The wave offering of the Jews seems to have been borrowed from Egypt, as it was a purely Egyptian custom, it consisted of waving before the deity a small metal stand, containing vegetables and flowers.

‡ Belmore Collection, plate 8.

§ For an example of this characteristic decoration, see the mummies in the Upper Egyptian Saloon, British Museum.

|| Belmore Collection, plate 12.

peated, differing only in this respect, that no votivi are presented, and the goddess, entirely serpentine, is resting on the outside

Fig. 54. Another, ditto ditto. These three tablets are fully described in the text.

of the shrine or pylon. In fig. 54 * Ranno is represented as a female figure, only so far ophite as to have a serpent's head. She is seated upon the ordinary throne of the gods, and in her right hand holds the peculiar cucufa staff, used by the male deities alone (the proper sceptre of the goddesses being a papyrus stem in blossom, with which they are usually represented); † the left hand of the deity appears to have been intended to clasp the ankh or cross of life.‡ A priest kneeling before the great goddess, shields his face with his hands while supplicating her favour. In fig. 55 § the subject represented is purely mythical, and forms part of the vignette to a funeral stelé.

Fig. 55. The god Chnum overcanopied by the goddess Ranno. (Same collection.)

This picture contains the Deity Chnuphis (fig. 55), or Kneph-Ra, the creating agency, || in the form of a ram-headed man, sitting

---

* Belmore Collection, plate 7.

† See an example in the British Museum, from the Wilkinson Collection, Case 1, Great Saloon.

‡ See for examples of both this sceptre and the ankh, the colossal statues of the goddess Pasht or Bubastis at the British Museum, Lower Saloon.

§ Belmore Collection.

|| Or Num, according to Dr. Birch.

in the sacred boat Baris, while the goddess Ranno (fig. 56), as a serpent, canopies him with her divine hypostasis, a sub-

Fig. 56. The sacred boat (Baris) of the sun, with the head of Amun, the supreme deity, encompassed by the serpent of goodness. (From the sarcophagus of Oimenepthah I.)

ject exactly similar to the vignette on the mummy-case of Aero Ai, before referred to, excepting that in this case the deity is Kneph-, and in the other, Horus-Ra. Both may probably idealize the same theory,—abstract immortality. It must, however, not be overlooked that, while in the case of Horus, Ranno wears the crown of the united kingdom, in that of Kneph-Ra she is coronated with the head-dress of Osiris,

Fig. 57. Sepulchral tablet representing the worship of the goddess Ranno. (Same collection.)

the avenger and judge of all men. In fig. 57,* which, like fig. 56, is defective, a priest is figured adoring Mersokar, the goddess of Upper Egypt, and presenting for her acceptance a tablet of cakes and bread. One remarkable peculiarity distinguishes this tablet: the goddess herself is not only drawn as a uræus, but her crest is surmounted by a head-dress formed of three uræi, each wearing the solar disk, as if to indicate a trinity of potentiality, or the junction of the offices of Isis, Nepthys, and Osiris, in her own person, three being, as is well known, the common Egyptian numerograph for completeness.

* Belmore Collection, plate 8.

Fig. 58,* the last and most singular state in the whole collection, is of a very different class to the preceding; and it is to be regretted that Egyptologists are not yet decided as to

Fig. 58. Adoration of an unknown species of coluber. (Same collection.)

its actual signification. Before a large and slender serpent, more resembling Apophis than any other of the mystic snakes of Egypt, kneels upon one knee an adoring worshipper. He is not, as in other instances, shielding or hiding his face with his hands, but is uplifting them in the usual attitude hieroglyphically adopted to signify the verb "to pray." The great snake itself is coiled in four upright convolutions, and appears to regard the suppliant with a majestic and not ungentle aspect. Although resembling Apophis (fig. 59), this reptile

Fig. 59. The cartouch containing the name of the last but one of the Hycsos kings, who was named Apophis after the great serpent of evil whom his predecessors worshipped.

cannot be identified with that monster, for there is no example of direct worship paid to the evil creature throughout

Fig. 60. Head of the serpent Apophis, with the hieroglyphics composing his name.

---

* Belmore Collection, plate 7.

the whole of Egyptian Mythology,* unless, indeed, we identify it with Sutekh, as the shepherd kings, the last but one of whom was named *Apophis* (fig. 60), appear to have done; and in that case the innovation led to a sanguinary revolution, which terminated the sway of the seventeenth dynasty, according to some chronologers 2214 B.C.† The probability, therefore, is that the adoration intended on this last tablet was offered to one of the household serpentine divinities analogous to that which obtained, in after-time, among the Romans, who, in all likelihood, derived it through the Etruscans, from the Egyptians themselves.‡ With respect to the kind of food offered in all these cases to serpent deities, Sir Gardner Wilkinson, in his

Fig. 61. The domestic snake of the Romans, with the altar containing a cluster of fruit. (From Gell and Gandy's *Pompeii.*)

great but imperfect, because *passé*, work, has a most interesting paragraph, which it will be only proper here to introduce.

"Ælian § relates many strange stories of the asp || and the respect paid to it by the Egyptians; but we may suppose that in his sixteen species of asps¶ other snakes were included.** He also speaks of a dragon, which was sacred in the Egyptian Melite, and another kind of snake called Paries or Paruas, dedicated to Æsculapius.†† The serpent of Melite had priests and ministers, a table and a bowl.‡‡ It was kept in a tower (fig. 61) and fed by the priests with cakes §§ made of flour and honey, which they placed there in the bowl. Having done this, they retired. The next day, on returning to the apart-

* Le Page Renouf, *ex. gr.*, in a letter to the author.

† Lenormant, *Ancient History*, vol. i. p. 197.

‡ *See* Gell and Gandy's *Pompeiana*, plate 76, for illustrations of mural paintings representing the Roman household serpents (Fig. 61.)

§ Ælian, x. 31, xi. 32, iv. 54.

|| Pliny, viii. 23.

¶ Ælian, x. 31.

** Ælian, xi. c. 17.

†† It is evident from Pausanias, that the dragon of the Greeks was only a large kind of snake, with, as he says, "scales like a pine cone."

‡‡ Ælian, viii. c. 19.

§§ Cakes seem to have been usually given to the snakes of antiquity, as to the dragon of the Hesperides.—*Æneid*, iv. 483.

ment, the food was found to be eaten, and the same quantity was again put into the bowl, for it was not lawful for any one to see the sacred reptile."*

"According to Juvenal,† the priests of Isis, in his time, contrived that the silver idols of snakes, kept in her temple, should move their heads to a supplicating votary."—*Ancient Egyptians*, vol. v. pp. 240-1.

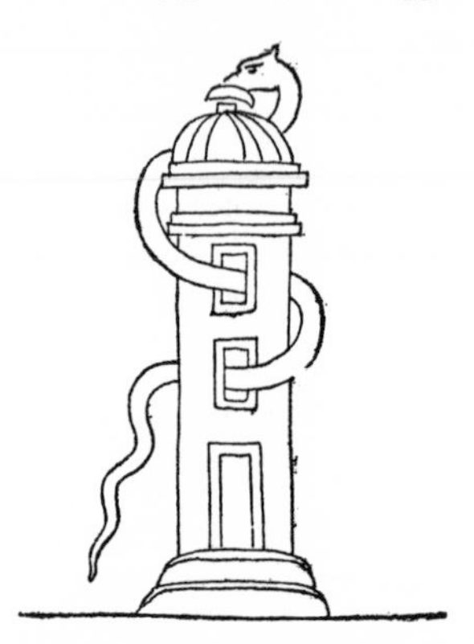

Fig. 62. The serpent in the tower. From a Gnostic gem. (Montfaucon.)

All this is in exact accordance with monumental evidence, and in harmony with one of the most curious of the Apocryphal books, the story of Bel and the Dragon.

12. Return we now to the serpent, the rise of whose myth is more immediately before us,—Apophis,‡ "the Destroyer." Prominent above all other species of reptile, a king among his genus, this baleful serpent twines his imbricated folds, as it were, around the stem of the ancestral tree of the Egyptian Theogony, and with brazen head and fiery eyes § stands forth in awful prominence. Vengeful and mysterious, always a malignant being, he was chosen to represent the very impersonation of spiritual, as his brother Typhon, or Baal, was of physical, evil. For the remainder then of this, not

* Cf. Ovid, lib. ii. *Amor.* Eleg. 13 to Isis: "Labatur circa donaria serpens."

† "Et movisse caput visa est argentea serpens."—Juvenal, *Sat. VI.* 537.
"Gently the silver serpent seems to nod."—Holyday's Translation.

"The silver snake
Abhorrent of the deed, was seen to quake."
Gifford's rendering.

‡ Apophis = אף-אף duplicate of אף *nose*, wrath, אנף foaming with rage (*anaph*).

§ The usual epithets applied to Apophis, in the Ritual of the Dead and the Litany of the Sun.

exhaustive but indicative, essay, his cultus claims, and must receive, our sole and best attention.* This fearful monster, called also the Giant, the Enemy, and the Devourer, was believed to inhabit the depths of that mysterious ocean upon which the Baris, or boat of the sun, was navigated by the gods through the hours of day and night, in the celestial regions. In not a few instances he was identified with Typhon,† the murderer of Osiris the (Rhot-Amenti, or judge of the dead), and the antagonist of Chefer-Ra, the benevolent creator, by whose son, the juvenile divinity

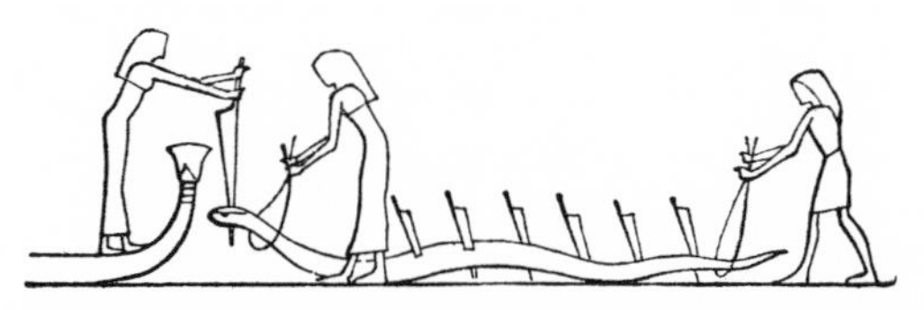

Fig. 63. The Osirian and the goddess Isis bringing Apophis wounded and bound to be slain in the head by Horus. Isis stands at the head, and the Osirian at the tail of Apophis. (Sharpe, Sar. Oimen.)

Horus (fig. 63), he is eventually overcome, aided by the united efforts of Isis, the Queen of Heaven, sister-consort of Osiris, and the twelve lesser deities of the heavenly powers. All this,

Fig. 64. The gods Set and Horus, united as *one* divinity, between the triple serpents of good. Executed prior to the time of the obliteration of all remains of the worship of Set, who was subsequently confounded with Apophis. (Sar. Oimen.)

---

* Occasionally Apophis is drawn with the crown of the lower kingdom upon his head, which, however, is not extraordinary, as the religion of the Delta had a great deal more of animal-worship in it than that of the Thebaid, and there the gods were venerated more from fear than love.

† In later Greco-Roman times, as in the earlier period, Apophis is also identified with Set, or Seth, the ass-headed deity of the Syrian or Hyesis tribes. One very late monument indeed speaks of "Seth, who is the Apophis of the waters."—Bunsen, i. 427.

and much more which is wholly inexplicable, is derived from perhaps the oldest of all uninspired liturgies, that most remarkable combination of prayers, incantations, and confessions, which extends over 166 chapters, and is called in hieroglyphy, "The Book of the Manifestation to Light," or the Ritual of the Dead. This work may be almost certainly traced back to the reign of Hesepti, of the first dynasty, according to Lenormant,* whose era is 5004 B.C., and to that of Menkera, the Mycerinus of Herodotus, of the fourth dynasty, 4325 B.C.† The names of both of these early Pharaohs occur in the text itself, although—and this is a most important incident to note—the final revision of the work, and a few additional chapters, were added as late as the period of Ethiopian conquest of Egypt, under the twenty-sixth dynasty, 665 B.C. Throughout this wonderful Ritual the idea of the serpent, as the soul of the world, and another variety of it, the Apophis, as the evil being, both antalogues of each other, occurs again and again, the soul has to arm itself against its machinations, and the body to be protected from its malignity. The deceased, when soul and body are reunited in the Amenti, or Egyptian Sheol, has to do combat with it, and the aid of every divinity is in turn invoked to overcome the enemy of the sun.‡ This will become still more apparent as we proceed to examine the Ritual, following the analysis of M. Lenormant and Dr. Birch, the while illustrating our examination by extracts from the mysterious document itself.

13. The opening chapter (1) of this ancient formulary is thus headed—"The beginning of the Chapters of the coming forth from the Day of bearing the Dead (spirits) in Hades (Kerneter) said on the day of the funeral . . . . by the (soul of) the Osirian deceased." In this prefatory portion of the Ritual, the deceased, addressing the deity of Hades, by the mouth of Thoth,§ the god of writing, enumerates all his claims to his favour, and asks for admittance into his dominions. Here at once appears the first indication of the contest against

---

* *Manual of the Ancient History of the East*, vol. i., whose chronology is a fair *via media* between the extravagancies of the French, and the incredulities of the English, school.

† The enormous antiquity ascribed by these authors to the Egyptian empire is neither generally accepted or even avowed, as the materials are still too few to fix a chronological table with any certainty.

‡ The modern Jews recite many blessings as they clothe themselves in the morning on rising, a system apparently borrowed from the Zendavesta Liturgy.—Anquetil du Perron, *Adoration of Ormuzd*.

§ Mercury, or Hermes Psychopompos, of the Greek Pantheon.

Apophis, the evil being, by the soul of the deceased exclaiming to the gods: "I have fought for *thee.* I come to expel the wicked [literally 'the opposers' of Satan the accuser] from Skhem (the heavenly region)." To this appeal the souls of the previously deceased, reply by interceding with Osiris for the admission of the applicant; speaking, as in the ancient idiom, of themselves in the third person, they exclaim: "Oh, companions of souls, made in the house of Osiris, accompany ye the soul of the Osirian, with yourselves, to the house of Osiris! Let him see as ye see; let him hear as ye hear; let him stand as ye stand; let him sit as ye sit! Oh, givers of food and drink to the spirits and souls made in the house of Osiris, give ye food and drink in due season to the Osirian with yourselves! Oh, openers of roads and guides of paths to the soul made in the abode of Osiris, open ye the roads, level ye the paths to the Osiris with yourselves!"* The result of this intercessional chorus is, that, "He enters the gate of Osiris; he is not found wanting in the balance; he goes in with exultation; he comes out (or passes through) in peace; he is like the demons in heaven; he is justified!"

14. After this grand exordium follow many short paragraphs (ii. to xiv.) of far less significance, relating chiefly to the body of the deceased, and the preliminary ceremonies of his funeral. These occupy the second to the fourteenth chapters. At last the soul of the deceased passes through the gates of the Kerneter (Hades), which, by the way, is a *subterranean* sphere, and at its entry is dazzled by the glory of the sun, which it now sees for the first time since its departure from the body (chap. xv.). Awe-struck with praise and admiration, thus the Osirian, or rather his soul, addresses the beneficent emblem of the Creator:—"Hail! Sun, Lord of the sunbeams, Lord of eternity! Hail! O Sun, Creator! self-created! Perfect is thy light in the horizon, illuminating the world with thy rays! All the gods rejoice when they see the King of Heaven! Glory to thee, shining in the firmament: thou hast shone, thou hast rendered it divine, making festive all countries, cities, and temples; supported by thy goodness; giving victory, first of the first; illuminating the Osirian in Hades, smiting the evil, placing him out of sin, and letting him be with the great blessed! Hail! thou judge of the gods, weighing words in Hades. Hail! thou who art over the gods. Hail! thou who

* Cf. Isaiah (xl. 3): "Prepare ye the way of the Lord; make straight in the desert a highway for our God."

hast cut in pieces the scorner, *and strangled the Apophis!* (Thou art the good peace of the souls of the dead!) * Oh! Creator, Father of the gods, incorruptible!" With this magnificent apostrophe concludes the first part of the Ritual.

15. In the second section of the book are traced the journeys and migrations of the soul in the lower region or Hades, to prepare it for which a long and complicated creed is introduced, forming the sixteenth chapter, or "the Egyptian faith." This section is accompanied, as indeed is every chapter, with a large vignette, representing the most sacred symbols of the mystic religion; and the text contains a description of these figures, with their mystical explanation. At first these are sufficiently clear, but, as they advance, a higher and more obscure region is reached; and, as it not unfrequently happens in theological works, the explanation ends by being more obscure than the symbols intended to be explained. This arises in a great measure from the rubrics added on to the text at a later date, probably in the nineteenth dynasty; and also to the esoteric, or magical invocations, which (by the same principle as the secreta in the Roman Missal) were ordered to be said privately by the embalmer on behalf of the deceased, and by the soul itself before the Hadean deities. In process of time these glosses and rubrics became confused with the Ritual, and by the ignorance of the Egyptian scribes, who had lost the knowledge of the sacred language they copied.† The confusion is thus rendered now almost inextricable. To make this apparent, a few sentences from the chapter shall here follow. The soul speaks, as before, sometimes in the third person, or else in the character of each of the principal divinites, by hypostatic union. The rubrics are here italicised, and the glosses printed in capitals. "I am the great God creating himself. IT IS WATER OR NU, WHO IS THE FATHER OF THE GODS. *Let him explain it.* I am yesterday [pre-existent eternity]. I know the morning [future eternity]. *Let him explain it.* YESTERDAY IS OSIRIS, THE MORNING THE SUN. The day on which are strangled the deriders of the universal lord. Soul of the Sun is his name! Begotten by Himself is his name! *Let him explain it.* I am the soul in two halves. *Let him explain it.* THE SOUL IN TWO HALVES IS THE SOUL OF THE SUN, AND THE SOUL OF OSIRIS. He (the soul) is conceived by Isis, engendered by Nepthys. Isis corrects his crimes, Nepthys cuts away his failings.

---

* Lenormant's rendering.

† As the modern Brahmin has that of the Vedic Sanscrit.

Millions of arms touch me, pure spirits approach me, evil-doers and all enemies avoid me; I live as I wished. *Let him explain it.*" It may a little clear off the obscurity of the preceding passages to quote, from another papyrus, "The soul, which dies like Osiris, rises again like the sun (Ra)." *

16. After the chapter on faith, follow a series of prayers to be pronounced during the process of embalming, whilst the body is being enveloped in its wrappers. These invocations are addressed to Thoth, who, as among the Greeks, performed the office of psychopompe, or conductor of souls. Throughout these are continual references to the mythic contest between Osiris and his half-brother Typhon, or Apophis, whom, by the assistance of his son, the mediator Horus, he finally overcomes, not however till he has himself upon this world been slain and dismembered by his opponent. Here, as elsewhere,

Fig. 65. Head of the goddess Typho, deity of gestation, with the usual feminine uræus. (Bunsen.)

Apophis, the great serpent, represents Typhon (fig. 65) as the evil principle, and the deceased implores, or rather the embalming priests do for him, that Thoth will assist him to assume the character of Horus, "the avenger of his father," that "his heart may be filled with delight, and his house be at peace before the head of the universal lord." To this petition the deity responds, "Let him go"; and the rubric adds: "This chapter being said, a person comes pure from the day he has been laid out, making all the transmigrations to place his heart. Should this chapter (have been attended to by him),† he (proceeds from above the earth,) he comes forth from all flame; no evil thing approaches him in pure clothes for millions of ages."

17. The body once wrapped in its coverings, and the soul well provided with a store of necessary knowledge, and able further to repeat and to explain the principles of the Egyptian faith, the deceased commences his journey; but as he is still

---

* Pierret, *Dogme de la Résurrection.* 1871.

† "Should this chapter have been inscribed or repeated over him."—Le Page Renouf. Or, "He goes forth upon the earth."—*Id.*

unable to move, and has not yet acquired the use of his limbs, it is necessary to address the gods, who successively restore all the faculties he possessed during life, so that he can stand upright, walk, speak, eat, and fight against the serpent Apophis, and his adherents. This process occupies chapters xxi. to xxix., which form the section called the "Reconstruction of the deceased." Osiris opens his mouth, gives him power to speak, restores his mind, &c.; and thus prepared he starts; he holds the pectoral scarabeus over his heart as a talisman, and then triumphantly passes from the gates of Hades, exclaiming as he does so: "I flourish upon earth; I never die in the west; I flourish as a spirit there for ever" (chap. xxx.).

18. From the first step, however, the actual conflict of the soul begins; terrible obstacles present themselves in its way; frightful Apophic monsters, servants of Typhon, crocodiles on land and in water, serpents of all kinds, tortoises, and other reptiles, more wild and terrible than Fuseli ever imagined, or Breughel drew, assail the deceased, and attempt to devour him.

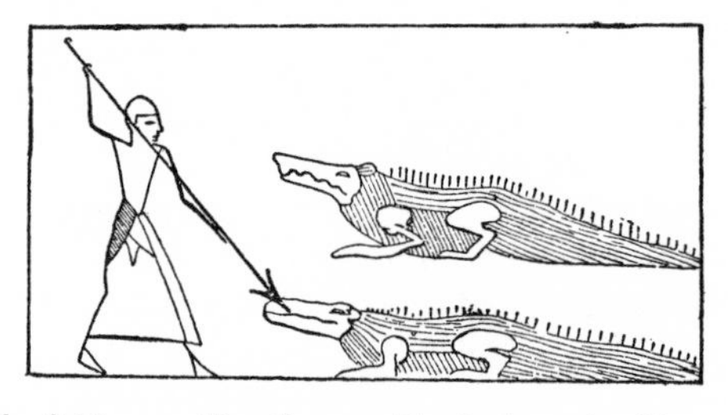

Fig. 66. The Osirian repelling the crocodiles in Amenti. (Sharpe, from the *Todtenbok* by Lepsius.)

19. First approaches the crocodile of Seb (fig. 66), whom he apostrophizes thus:—

"Stop, go back, O crocodile, from coming to me. I know thee by my spells. Thou darest not speak the name of the great God,* because I myself have come. I perceive, I prevail, I judge; I have defended myself; I have sat in the birthplace of Osiris; born with him, I renew myself like him."—Bunsen's translation, chap. xxxi.

"Back, crocodile Hem, back, crocodile Shui. Come not against me. I

* The mystic name of deity among the Greeks, or the Tetragrammaton, was likewise not allowed to be uttered. The Jews have a similar notion concerning the word יהוה, which they asserted enabled Jesus to perform all his miracles, by stealing the pronunciation of it from the high priest while playing in the temple area.

have knowledge of potent spells. Utter not the name of the great God."—Renouf's translation.

By these adjurations the crocodile is repelled.

20. Four other crocodiles now approach, one from each quarter of the world; but these are also driven back by the Osirian, with the following precations:—

"My father saves me from the eight crocodiles. Back, crocodile of the west, living off those that never rest, I am not given to thee. Back, crocodile in the east, do not turn me, I have not been given to thee. Back, crocodile of the south, living off the unclean, do not gore me with thy claw, I am not given to thee. Back, crocodile of the north, spit thou thy venom away from my head, I am not given to thee. My face is open, my heart is in its place, my head is on me daily; I am the sun creating himself, no evil thing injures me" (chap. xxxii.).

21. These driven away, a viper approaches the Osirian, which, with a spear, he turns back, addressing it thus:—

Fig. 67. The Osirian repelling the viper Ru in Amenti. (Sharpe, as above.)

"O walking viper, makest thou Seb and Shu (the deities) stop. Thou hast eaten the abominable rat of the sun; thou hast devoured the bones of the filthy cat" (chap. xxxiii.).

Or—

"O viper Ru, advance not. Mine is the virtue of Seb and Shu. Thou hast eaten the rat which the sun abominates."*

22. Other combats follow; the deceased and the reptiles, against which he contends, mutually insulting and menacing each other in a perfectly Homeric fashion. At last, in the 39th chapter, a serpent sent forth from Apophis attacks him, breathing out venom and fire, but in vain; with his weapon the Osirian repels the reptiles, accompanying the action with these words:—

"Back, thou precursor, the sent forth from Apophis; thou shalt be

---

* This is the literal rendering of a passage, which means simply, "I am Seb and Shu."—Renouf.

drowned in the pool of the firmament, where thy father has ordered thee to be cut up. Back, block of stone, thy destruction is ordered for thee by ruth (Thmei). The precursors of Apophis, the accusers of the sun are o verthrown."

23. Thus baffled, the terrible serpent would withdraw; but he is not thus to escape punishment, for the deceased, assuming the character of each of the lesser gods in turn, assists them to loosen the ropes from the back of the sun, and therewith to bind the Apophis. Other deities, with snares

Fig. 68. The gods holding Apophis back. (Sar. Oimen.)

and nets, search the celestial lake in pursuit of the hideous reptile (fig. 68), whom at last they find, and whose struggles

Fig. 69. The hand of Amun restraining the malevolence of Apophis. (Sar. Oimen.)

would overturn the boat of the sun, and immerse the deities in the water, if it were not for an enormous mystic hand (fig. 69) (that of Amun), which, suddenly arising from the

Fig. 70. Another vignette representing the same subject. (Sar. Oimen.)

depths below, seizes the rope, and thus secures the Evil One (fig. 70). Once fastened, Horus wounds the snake in the head with his spear,* while the deceased and the

* Here the mythic contests of Vishnū and the great serpent Caliya, in Hindū theology, will at once occur to the recollection of the reader.

guardian deities, standing upon its voluminous folds, stab the Apophic monster with knives and lances (fig. 71).*

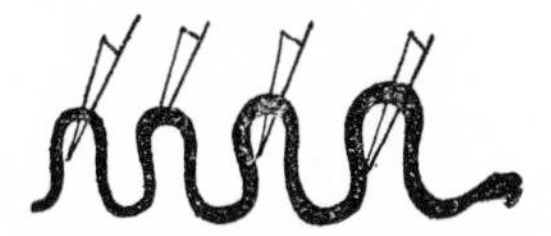

Fig. 71. Apophis transfixed by knives. (Sar. Oimen.)

Wounded, tortured, and a prisoner, the great snake is at last destroyed and annihilated,† and the boat of the sun shortly after attains the extreme limit of the horizon, and disappears in the heavenly region of Amenti, or the west.‡ It has been necessary a little to anticipate this struggle of good against evil, the origin of the Persian dualistic system, and the Ophite Gnostic heresy, necessary, because the soul of the deceased, in the character of the gods, performs these avenging acts, and in the taunting speeches which preface them, declares the supreme sovereignty of *one* Divine being,§ the creator alike of good and evil, the rewarder of all the just, and the ultimate annihilator of the wicked. This prefaced, the following extracts from the 39th chapter of the Ritual will now become intelligible. It is the soul who is accosting the baffled Apophis, and prophetically foretelling his future conquest of it by speaking in the past and present tenses.

"I act peaceably for thee, O sun; I make the haul of thy rope, O sun. The Apophis is overthrown; the cords of all the gods bind the south, north, east, and west. Their cords are on him. Victory, the sphinx, has overthrown him; the god Harubah has knotted him. The Apophis and accusers of the sun fall, overthrown is the advance of Apophis. [To Apophis]: Thy tongue is greater than the envious tongue of a scorpion which has been made to thee; it has failed in its power for ever. Back, thy hard head is cut; the gods drag thy limbs and cut thy arms. [To Horus]: O Horus, the water of the sun is stopped by thee. The great Apophis, the accusor of the sun, has been judged by Akar. (?) Lift ye up your good faces. The wicked one has been stopped by the assembled gods; he has been received by Nu (the deity Chnuphis). He stands, and the great gods are victors towing him. Athor and the gods drag him exhausted, avenging the sun four times [an Egyptian idiom, signifying perfectly] against the Apophis."||

---

* Bonomi, *Sarcophagus of Oimenepthah I.*, Plates 2, 3, 7, and 8.

† Cf. Isaiah xxvii. 1; Rev. xii. 9; Job xxvi. 13.

‡ Champollion, *Lettres écrites sur l'Egypte*, 1833, p. 232.

§ "I make peace and create evil."—Isaiah xlv. 7.

|| The whole of this chapter is dreadfully corrupt, and unintelligible except by bits.—Renouf.

24. After this triumphant victory, the deceased, or rather his soul, breaks out into a song of triumph. He declares himself to be identical with the great gods, and likens the members of his body to those of the gods to whom they are dedicated, and by whom they are protected. He even boasts that he has the strength of Typhon, whom he has overthrown, and thus he declares his members to be dedicated, and equal, to those of the following deities:—

The Dedication of different parts of the body (chap. xlii.).

My	Hair is in shape (au) that of			Nu.*
,,	Face	,,	,,	Ra.
,,	Eyes	,,	,,	Athor.
,,	Ears	,,	,,	Spheru.
,,	Nose	,,	,,	Khentskhem.
,,	Lips	,,	,,	Anup.
,,	Teeth	,,	,,	Selk.
,,	Neck	,,	,,	Isis.
,,	Arms	,,	,,	Lord of Tattu (the soul).
,,	Elbows	,,	,,	Neith, of Sais.
,,	Legs	,,	,,	Mentu, of Khar.
,,	Belly and Back		,,	Seb, or Thoth.
,,	Spine	,,	,,	Acht.
,,	Phallus	,,	,,	Osiris.
,,	Thigh	,,	,,	Eye of Horus.
,,	Legs (2)	,,	,,	Nu.
,,	Feet	,,	,,	Pthah.
,,	Arms	,,	,,	Her Heft, or Sheft (the ram-headed)
,,	Fingers and Nails		,,	Living Uræi.

There is not a limb of him (the Osirian) without a god. He it is who comes out sound: immortal is his name. He dies not again. He is escaped from all evil things. He is Horus (in his capacity of the destroyer of Apophis), who lives amongst millions.

(This chapter concludes the section entitled the Preservation of the Body in Hades.)

25. After these exhausting labours the Osirian needs rest, and for a while he waits in Amenti to recruit his strength, and satisfy his hunger (chaps. xliii. to lvi.). He has escaped great dangers, and has not gone astray in the mystic desert,

---

* The verb *au* may be either indicative or subjunctive. I believe the context requires it to be subjunctive, and that all this is a prayer thus: "Let the hair of the Osirian be that of Nu (or become Nu) . . . . Let there not be a limb of him without a god."—Renouf.

where he would have died of hunger and thirst (chaps. li.—liii.). At last he reaches the sacred sycamore, or tree of life,* in the

Fig. 72. The goddess Nu in the sacred sycamore-tree, pouring out the water of life to the Osirian and his soul, represented as a bird, in Amenti. (Sharpe, from a funereal stelē in the British Museum.)

midst of the boughs of which the goddess Nu† (fig. 72) is stationed. She, pitying his exhausted condition, and anxious to aid his further progress, gives him heavenly bread, with supernatural virtues of sustentation, and a fluid which is expressly termed "the water of life." This having drunk, grateful and refreshed, the Osirian exclaims, "I grow, I live, I breathe again!" and prepares to recommence his journey to reach the first gate of heaven.‡

26. Then commences a long dialogue between the deceased and the personification of the divine light, who instructs him in a chapter called the Manifestation to Light (chap. lxiv.). This dialogue presents a most remarkable resemblance to the dialogue prefixed to the books given by the Alexandrian Greeks as translations of the ancient religious writings of Egypt, between Thoth (Hermes Trismegistus) and the Light, the latter explaining to Thoth the most sublime mysteries of nature. This portion is certainly one of the best and grandest of the Ritual, and is doubtless the source of all that is mystical and profound in the so-called Hermetic books of the later Platonists.§

27. The Osirian having passed the first gate, continues to advance, guided by this new light, to whom, in the lxv^th^ to the lxxv^th^ chapters, he addresses his invocations. He then

---

* The tree of life is sometimes represented as a persea, or peach-tree, groves of which formerly adorned the inner courts of many Egyptian temples, and the last specimen of which in Egypt existed till very lately in the garden of a convent at Cairo, but has been recently wantonly destroyed.

† Wilkinson, vol. i. p. 391. ‡ Lenormant, *in loco.*

§ *Ritual,* cap. lix.

enters on a series of transformation, more and more elevated, assuming the form of, and identifying himself with, the noblest divine symbols. He is changed successively into a hawk, emblem of Horus-Ra (chap. lxxvii.); an angel, or a divine messenger (chaps. lxxix., lxxx.); into a lotus (lxxxi.); the "pure lily which comes out of the fields of the sun"; into the god Pthah (lxxxii.), in which hypostasis he declares "he is stronger than the lord of many years"; into a kind of crested heron, the sacred bird of Osiris, called Bennu (chap. lxxxiii.), whose residence is on the boughs of the tree of life; into a crane, or a species of nycticorax (chap. lxxxiv.); into a human-headed bird,* the most usual of all emblematic representations of the soul, a bird, moreover, occasionally represented as furnished with human hands, which it holds up in adoration to the sun (chap. lxxxv.); into a swallow (chap. lxxxvi.), in which latter form the soul utters this remarkable expression, "O great one, I have dissipated my sins; I have destroyed my failings, for I have got rid of the sins which detained me upon earth"; next into a *serpent*, the soul of the earth; and here, although in one form the serpent of the earth is confounded with Apophis, in another it is distinct, a circumstance which has misled many students in comparative mythology. As the chapter (lxxxvii.) is a short one, it will be as well to re-insert it entire.

"I am the serpent Ba-ta† (*not* Apophis), [or 'Sata (the serpent) of long years, in the extremities of the earth.'—Renouf,] soul of the earth, whose length is years, laid out and born daily; I am the soul of the earth in the parts of the earth; I am laid out and born, decay and become young daily." (See *suprà*, fig. 39.)

28. The last transformation of the Osirian is into another reptile; the first of those which on entering Hades he overcame, viz. a crocodile (chap. lxxxviii.) no longer "the eater of filth and the opposer of the souls," but the crocodile "who dwells in victories, whose soul comes from men, the great fish (or rather reptile) of Horus." Up to this time the soul of the deceased has been making its journeys alone, it has been merely a sort of εἴδωλον (eidolon), that is an image—a shade with the appearance of the body which yet lay torpid and sensationless. After these transformations, the soul becomes reunited to the body which it will need for the rest of its journey. This theory it was which rendered the process of mummification so important, for it was indispensable that the

* The souls of kings are generally furnished with crowns, as *vide* numerous examples in the Hay collection.

† Bata, *Brass of Earth.*—Dr. Birch.

soul upon its return should find its former residence well and sacredly preserved. "O," cries the body by a sublime paronomasia, "that in the dwelling of the master of life I may be reunited to my glorified soul. Do not order the guardians of Heaven to destroy me, so as to send away my soul from my corpse, and hinder the eye of Horus, who is with thee, from preparing may way" (chap. lxxxix.). The vignette to this chapter is one of the most usual in Egyptian hieroglyphy; it represents the embalmed body laid upon a bier, having under it the four vases for the eviscerated organs; at the side of the couch stands Anubis, the guardian of the dead, preparing the body for its revivification, while above flies a

Fig. 73. The ankh, or crux ansata, from the very earliest periods the hieroglyph for life, originally supposed to have been an earring.*

human-headed bird, having in one talon the ankh (fig. 73), or tau cross, and in the other a mast and expanded sail, the ideographs for "breath" and life respectively.

29. The deceased traverses next the dwelling of Thoth, who presents him with a roll containing further instructions for his safe progress, and fresh lessons of the heavenly knowledge he is soon to require (chap. xc.). Armed with these, the Osirian arrives on the banks of the subterranean river, separating him from the Elysian fields of Amenti; but there a new danger awaits him. A false boatman, the emissary of the Typhonic Powers (in this instance distinct from Apophis), lays wait for him on his way, and endeavours by deceitful words to get him into his boat, so as to mislead, and take him to the east instead of to the west (chap. xciii.), his proper destination, the shore where he ought to land and rejoin the sun of the lower world. Fortified by his previous instructions, the Osirian again escapes this subtle danger; he remarks the perfidy of the false messenger, and repulses him with bitter reproaches. At last he meets the right vessel to conduct him to his destination (chaps. xcvii., xcviii.); and now in sight of the true boat; over the unknown and fathomless river, he declares that he is prepared "to pass from earth to heaven, to go along to the ever tranquil gods, when they go to cut the Apophis." "I," he con-

* From its sign also being the determinative hieroglyphic of everything pertaining to the ear.

tinues, "I have brought the ropes, stopping the wicked (one) as I go along in the boat of Pthah; I have come from the scalding pools, from the flaming fields, alive from the great pool."*

30. Ere, however, the Osirian can enter the boat of Pthah, it is necessary to ascertain if he is really capable of making the voyage, if the deceased possesses a sufficient amount of the knowledge necessary to his safety, and which he is supposed to have obtained from the papyri presented to him by Thoth. The divine boatmen accordingly proposes a series of questions to his passenger, who declares he has come to see his father Osiris, (having, as before stated, taken the nature and form of Horus,) and to fight the Apophis. This reply satisfies the interlocutor, who bids him "go to the boat, which will carry him to the place he knoweth where." Here a most curious and mystical scene ensues, for each part of the vessel becoming animated, requests the Osirian to "tell me my name," that is, the esoteric meaning of it. Anchor, paddle, mast, poop, hull, planking, all in turn accost, and are in turn replied to, for twenty-three questions and answers; which finished, the deceased entreats the "good beings, lords of truth, who are living for ever, circling for ever," to pass him through "the waters, to give him to eat food, and baked cakes, and a place in the hall of the two truths before the great God." In the hundredth chapter the Osirian, having declared again that he has "stopped the Apophis and turned back its feet," is permitted to embark, and safely crossing the mighty river, lands on the other bank in the land of the mountains of the west, the blessed country of Amenti.

Fig. 74. One of the mystic crocodiles of Amenti, named Shesh-shesh. (Sar. Oimen.

31. Here commence another series of chapters, containing descriptions of and an abstract of the geography of the spirit-land; and here again, as usual in the Ritual, the Ophite myth is interwoven throughout. The blessed region is described as "the valley of Balot,† or abundance, at the end of

---

* It would be superfluous to do more here than refer to the Greek myths of Hades, Styx, Charon and his boat, and to the mediæval legend of St. Patrick's purgatory, as given in the History of Roger de Wendover; their almost exact analogy is too obvious to be dwelt upon.

† Called more properly the "Valley of Buchat."—Renouf.

heaven, 370 cubits long and 140 broad." In a cavern in one of the holy mountains is the great crocodile Sabak * (chap. cviii.), and at the head of the valley extends an enormous snake thirty cubits long and six in circumference. His head is of stone,† and is three cubits broad, and the name of the terrible supernatural is "Eater of fire." On coming near to this guardian genius, for such the serpent is, the Osirian in secret assumes the character of a similar reptile, and declares "he is the serpent the son of Nu," and presently he boasts that he has "taken the viper of the sun as he was resting at evening," and "that the great snake has coiled round the heaven." Further, "that he is ordered to approach the sun, as the sun is setting from the land of life to his horizon"; that "he knows the passage of spirits, the arrest of the Apophis in it." This seems to be, as nearly as may be guessed, the meaning of this chapter (cviii.), which is one of the most confused in the Ritual.

32. In the next chapter (cix.) is a further description of the heavenly region, on the north of which is a lake called the Lake of Primordial Matter,‡ a chaos in fact; and on the south the lake of Sacred Principles, possibly spiritual essences. In chapter cx. the land of Amenti is further described as a magnified kingdom of Egypt, with its lakes, canals, palaces, fields, &c. There the walls are of iron, and the corn grows seven cubits high. There the sycamore-trees (trees of life)

Fig. 75. The god Nilus or Hapimou encircled by the serpent of eternal years. Possibly the heavenly Nile is here represented. (Wilkinson.)

are of copper, and there the spirits of the blest are dwelling, and the sun shines for ever. In this delightful climate for

---

* After whom Sabakoph, the Ethiopian, mentioned in 2 Kings xvii. 4, under the name of So, was named. The name is there written סוא.

† An idiom for extreme hardness, a peculiarity common to the frontal plates of certain species of vipers.

‡ Incidentally, the great antiquity of the Ritual is proven by its continual reference to lakes. Seas or oceans, such as the peninsular Hellenes delighted in, do not occur in the mythology of the Egyptians, who, up to the time of Thothmoses, were not aware of the existence of the Atlantic, nor till that of Necho, thought otherwise than that the Mediterranean was a vast lake.

Fig. 76. The Judgment scene in the Hall of the Two Truths. (Taken from a papyrus first engraved by Denon. See next page.)

THE JUDGMENT BY OSIRIS IN THE HALL OF THE TWO TRUTHS.—The first part of this vignette, from an ancient papyrus, represents the mystic weighing, and the second part the intercession, before Osiris. 1. Isis, the Queen of Heaven, who, together with (3) Horus-Ra, introduces the deceased (2) into the Hall of Judgment. In the centre of the picture stands the balance (4), in one scale of which (5) is the heart of the deceased, and in the other a weight (6) in the form of the goddess of Truth ; behind the balance is the entrance to hell, guarded by a Typhocerberic monster (7) ; Anubis (8), the guardian of the dead, adjusts the beam, while Thoth (9) records the result upon his tablet. This ends the first scene. In the second part of the picture, Horus-Ra, crowned with the Pschent (11), introduces and pleads for the deceased (10), now invested with the robe of Justification. Before Osiris (13) are the four genii of the body upon an altar of lotus-flowers, being offered as intercessors for the Osirian, their office being specially to plead for the sins committed by that part of the body over which they individually presided. Behind Osiris stand the goddesses Isis and Nepthys, waiting to conduct the justified Osirian into the regions of Amenti.

awhile the Osirian dwells, sowing corn, ploughing with heavenly oxen, and reaping the harvest in the Elysian fields. It was for this purpose that a hoe and a basket full of corn were buried with every Egyptian, that in the future life he might not be unprepared to follow his agricultural labours. There the Osirian freely, and frequently, partakes of the bread of knowledge, which he is shortly to find more necessary than ever, as he has arrived at the end of all his trials but *one*, and that one the last and most terrible, for as yet he is only in a superior kind of *Sheol*, or Hades, undergoing a purification,

Fig. 77. The avenging Assessor watching to punish the Osirian. (Papyrus, British Museum.)

as in Hades itself his soul was subjected to purgatorial influence conducted by Anubis, the guardian of the dead, the Osirian traverses an unknown labyrinth (chaps. cxiii. to cxxi.); but by the aid of a clue and the assistance of Thoth, he penetrates through all its intricacies and windings, and at last is ushered into the judgment-hall, where Osiris Rhot-Amenti,*

Fig. 78. The snake-headed Assessor standing to interrogate the Osirian. (Wilkinson.

the judge of the dead, awaits him seated on his throne, surrounded as by a jury, with a court of forty-two assessors, four of whom are serpent-headed (figs. 77, 78). There the

* Whence the Greek name of Pluto, Rhadamanthus, was doubtless derived.

decisive sentence is to be pronounced, either admitting the deceased to happiness, or excluding him for ever (chap. cxxv.).

33. On a raised throne before the Osirian, sits the awful deity Osiris, upon whose head are the double crowns of the united kingdoms of Upper and Lower Egypt, circled with the solar asp or uræus. In his hands are the cross of life, the Cucufa staff of dominion, the curved lituus* denoting sacerdotal authority, and the scourge of Khem. Behind his throne are the avenging Cabereii, children of Typhon or Set, and his consort the hippopotamus-headed goddess (Thoeris) of hell; lastly, underneath his feet, fettered and tortured, lie the souls of the condemned.† Lest the Osirian should quail and be unable to stand before the solemn assembly, the goddesses Isis and Nepthys, deities of the upper and lower firmament respectively, support his trembling footsteps, while Amset, Tautmutf, Kabhsenuf, and Hapi, the guardian deities of the dead, intercede for his protection. On an altar before them, flowers and incense burn in fragrant propitiation, and between it and the judge, in a massive and yet delicate balance, the heart of the deceased is weighed against the feather of Thmei, the goddess of Truth. Thoth, the introducer of spirits, writes down the preponderance of the weight for good or evil, while an ape (the emblem of justice because all his extremities are even), sitting on the summit of the cross-beam, prevents either fraud or favour. Now is the Osirian to give an account of his whole former life, and while each of the forty-two assessors accuses him of some flagrant fault, he has in return to reveal to the questioner his own secret name, and to profess his innocence of the fault alleged. This is called the apology, or the negative confession, and it is one of the most sublime and singular ethical formularies in the whole of ancient mythology. The first part of this address is negative; but as heaven to the Egyptians was not accessible by mere sinlessness, but was the reward only of active virtue, the Osirian, from the evils he has not done, proceeds to the enumeration of the good which he has performed, and entreats not the clemency, but the equity, of the Judge. Extending then his arms towards the deity, thus he addresses the adjudicator Osiris and his coadjutor divinities:—

"O ye Lords of truth, O thou Great God, Lord of truth, I have come to thee, my Lord, I have brought myself to see thy blessings; ‡ I have known

* Is this the origin both of the Druidical lituus and the episcopal staff?
† Not always represented on the funeral Papyri. See Sar Oimen. pl. 5.
‡ For "blessings" read "splendid glories."—Renouf.

thee, I have known thy name, I have known the names of the forty-two of the gods who are with thee in the hall of the Two Truths, who live by catching the wicked, and feeding off their blood, in the day of reckoning of words, before the good being, the justified.*

"Rub ye away my faults,† for I have not privily done evil against mankind, neither have I afflicted persons or men ; I have not told falsehoods before the tribunal of truth, I have had no acquaintance with evil, I have not done any wicked thing, I have not made the labouring man perform more than his daily task, I have not been idle, I have not failed, I have not been weak (*in the sense of sinful*), I have not done what is hateful to the gods, I have not calumniated the slave to his master, I have not sacrificed (*filled the office wrongfully of a priest*), I have not murdered, I have not given orders to smite a person privily, I have not done fraud to any man, neither have I altered the measures of the country. I have not injured the images of the gods, I have not withheld milk from the mouths of sucklings, neither have I netted the sacred fish ;‡ I have not stopped running water, I have not robbed the gods of their offered haunches, I have not caused to weep, I have not multiplied words in speaking, I have not blasphemed a god, I have not made a conspiracy, I have not corrupted women or men, neither have I polluted myself; I have not stolen from the dead, I have not played the hypocrite, I have not caused any to weep, I have not despised any god in my heart ; I am pure, I am pure—let no harm happen to me from the avenging genii ; save, O save me from them.

"O Lords of truth, I have made to the gods the offerings due unto them, I have given food to the hungry, I have given drink to the thirsty, I have given clothes to the naked,§ I have been attentive to the words of truth, I am pure from all sins, I am free from the curse of the wicked, I have done what the gods writ upon earth, I have no sins, and no perversion—place me before thyself, O Lord of Eternity, and let me pass through the roads of darkness and dwell with thee for ever."

34. To so magnificent an appeal, and to a soul so consciously perfect, but one answer can the deity return. At a signal from Osiris, the deceased is invested in a long white linen robe,||

---

* "I have brought to you truth, and have blotted out your iniquity."—*Id.*

† The first clause, literally *un nefer*, may really be not an address but a proper name.—*Id.*

‡ The Lepidotus, or Oxyrhynchus Niloticus, worshipped at Latopolis as a form of the goddess Athor. — Wilkinson's *Ancient Egyptians*, vol. ii. pp. 248—251.

§ After naked occurs, in some papyri, the further clause, "and a boat to the shipwrecked."—Renouf.

|| A specimen of this garment in the Hay collection measured 16 feet by 9, and was furnished with a broad twisted fringe along the outer edge. The name for this garment among the ancient Egyptians was "Basoui."

fringed with a symbolical fringe along one side of it (the origin possibly of the Jewish arbang kanphoth,* ארבע כנפות) and then, while Thoth writes the decree of acquittal upon the rolls of Heaven, the deity and assessors, jointly addressing the Osirian, exclaim, "Go forth, thou who hast been introduced. Thy food is from the eye of God, thy drink is from the eye of God, thy meats are from the eye of God. Go thou forth, O Osirian, justified for ever."

35. After the confession (cxxv.) commences the third part of the Ritual, or the Adoration of the Sun. The chapters in this are more mystical and obscure than any of the preceding. The Osirian, henceforth identified with the sun, traverses with him, and as he, the various houses of heaven, fighting again with the Apophis, and ascending to the lake of celestial fire, the antipodes of the Egyptian hell,† and the source of all light. In its closing chapters the work rises to a still more mystical and higher practical character, and the deceased is finally hypostated into the form of every sacred animal and divinity in the Egyptian Pantheon, and with this grand consummation the Ritual closes. But even in heaven itself the serpent myth is dominant. Not only does the deceased, as the sun, declare

Fig. 79. The Osirian endeavouring to snare the giant Apophis; above his head, as protecting him in his dangerous task, is the winged orb, symbolic of divine interpenetration and assistance. (Sar. Oimen.)

"that he puts forth blows against the Apophis (fig. 79), strangling the wicked in the west" (chap. cxxvi.), but even in the

---

* See Mill's *The British Jews*.

† What this fearful lake was may be gathered from the following description of the Egyptian Hell.

"Oh! the place of waters—none of the dead can stand in it, its water is of fire, its flow is of fire, it glows with smoking fire; if wished, there is no drinking it. The thirst of those who are in it is inextinguishable. Through the greatness of its terror, and the magnitude of its fear, the gods, the deceased, and the spirits, look at its waters from a distance. Their thirst is inextinguishable; they have no peace; if they wish, they cannot escape it."—*Ritual*, chap. cl. xiii. above.

highest heaven the house of Osiris is entered only by seven pylons, each guarded by an uræus, or sacred asp; the name of the first guardian being "Sut or Set"; of the second, "Fire-face"; of the third, "Vigilant"; of the fourth, "Stopper of

Fig. 80. The serpent warder of the gateway of the path of the sun; behind are Horus-Ra, and possibly the serpent Ranno. (Sar. Oimen.)

many Words"; of the fifth, "Consumer"; the sixth, "Stone-face"; and of the seventh, "Stopper of the Rejected,"—all epithets applied to the snake, and sometimes even to Apophis. The next abode of Osiris has twenty-one gates, each containing a different deity (the eighth being a double snake-headed god), armed with swords to destroy the impious intruder. Each of these in turn the Osirian supplicates; and by each he is bidden to pass on, for "thou art justified." Next is approached another abode, entered through fifteen pylons, each surmounted by one, two, or more snakes armed as before, whose names, and that of the snakes, are as follows:—1. Mistress of Terror, and the snake "Vulture"; 2. Mistress of Heaven, and the snake "born of Pthah"; 3. Mistress of Altars, and the snake

Figs. 81, 82. Two more of the mistresses, the lion- and cow-headed respectively.

Fig. 81. "Her name is Skab the Subduer."

Fig. 82. "Her name is Sehneka, or Beater of the Bulls."

"Subduer" (fig. 81); 4. Hard-man, regent of earth, and the snake "Bull-smiter" (fig. 82); 5. Fire, mistress of the breath of the nostril, and the snake "Retainer of the Profane"; 6. Mistress of Generations, and the snake "Conspirator"; * 7. the Gate of Ruin, and the snake "Destroyer"; 8. Gate of Inextinguishable Fire, and the snake "Protector of the Sacred Eye"; 9. Mistress of Limbo (figs. 83, 84, 85), and the snake "Pride"; 10. Gate of Loud Words, and the snake "Great Clasper"; 11. Gate of Hard-face, and the snake "Terrifier"; 12. Gate of the

The Mistresses or Doorkeepers of Amenti, with the great Uræus above. (Ritual, cap. cxlv–vi.)

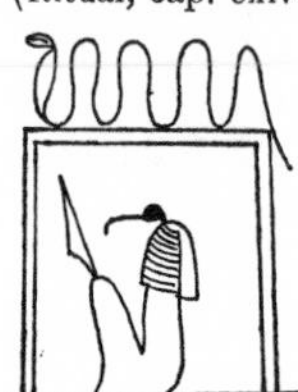

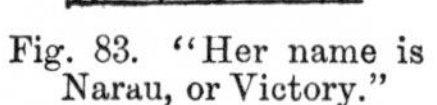

Fig. 83. "Her name is Narau, or Victory." 84. "Her name is Han-nekah, or Commanding the idle." 85. "Her name is Mes-Pthah, or born of Pthah."

Questioner of Earth; 13. Gate of Isis? 14. Mistress of Exultation; 15. Gate of Souls of the Red-haired. The names of the snakes of the four last gates are not given. To these abodes succeed (chap. cxlviii.) seven staircases, whose guardians have the same names as the snakes of the seven gates. Then the Osirian passes to the fourteen abodes of Elysium, in the fourth of which, "on the very high hill in Hades,—the heaven rests upon it," occurs a "snake—Sati is his name. He is

Fig. 86. Ruhak, the great charmer whom the sun has made. (Ritual cap. cxlix.)

about seventy cubits in his coil, and he lives by decapitating the condemned."† In the seventh abode dwells a similar snake,—"Ruhak is its name (fig. 87). He is about seven cubits

---

* Is this an allusion to the Indo-Germanic myth of the connection between life and fire?—See Cox's *Mythology of the Aryan Nations*; and Kelly, *Indo-Germanic Folk-lore.*

† Is this an exaggeration of the great African rock-snake (*Python regia*), who, by the way, resembles in a remarkable degree the Egyptian figures of Apophis.

in the length of his back, living off the dead, strangling their spirits." Him the Osirian beseeches—

"Draw thy teeth, weaken thy venom, or thou dost not pass by me. Do not send thy venom to me, overthrowing and prostrating me through it."

Or, more properly, "Be thy teeth broken, and thy venom weakened; come not against me, emit not thy venom against me, overthrowing and prostrating (me) through it." (Renouf.) Finally, at the door of the sixteenth abode resides another snake, at the mouth of the heavenly Nile, who is pacified by offerings of food and grain. Other magical addresses follow these, and the rubric of the last chapter ends thus:— "This book is the greatest of all mysteries; do not let the

Fig. 87. Wooden votive figure of the goddess Urhapt. (From a statue in the British Museum, restored by the help of a similar figure in the Leyden Museum.)

eye of any one see it, that is detestable. Learn it, hide it, make it. The Book of the Ruler of the Secret Place is it named. It is ended."*

36. Such, then, is a summary of the contents of the most ancient ritual extant. From it have probably been derived all the later systems of Ophiolatry, as in its pages are preserved the deflected echoes of a primitive revelation. Possessing extraordinary coincidences with later dogmas, there is yet little doubt that the condition of the work as we now have it is one of great and wilful mutilation—whole chapters are inverted, and sentences misconstrued. Nor can the result be wondered at when it is recollected that, to quote Professor Lyell,† no language is extant after a lapse of a thousand years,

---

* Ruhak or Urtuk is, as before mentioned, occasionally represented as a goddess in the form of an upright uræus, with its tail coiled in a kind of bow-knot for a pedestal. Several votivi, in wood, to this goddess are in the British Museum, Cases 10 and 11, Upper Egyptian Saloon.

† *Elements of Geology.*

and the Ritual of the Dead was used and written in ancient Egypt for more than thirty centuries.*

37. Apart, however, from the Ritual, the trail of the serpent is as conspicuous on the monumental history of Egypt as it is

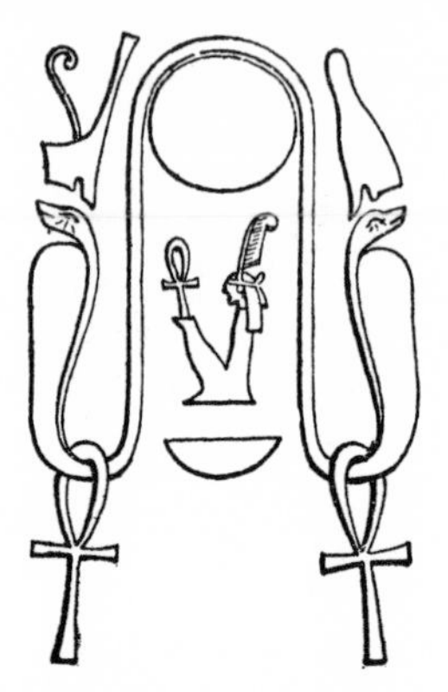

Fig. 88. The solar orb with the emblematic figure of the goddess Thmei, or Truth, between the sacred uræi. (Cassell.) See fig. 40.

in the archæographic. Every sepulchral stelè or funereal slab bore at its upper extremity the usual winged disc of Ra, with its pendent basilisks (fig. 88), wearing the alternate crowns of

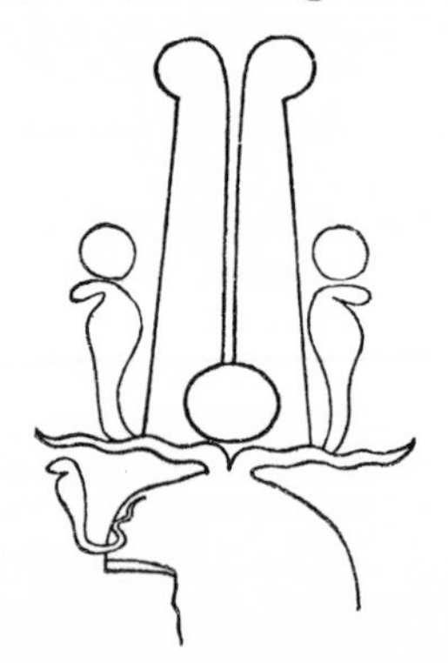

Fig. 89. The royal and sacred head-dresses united.

Upper and Lower Egypt and the cross of life. Not unfrequently the god Ra, and even the King himself, as that deity's incarnation, is represented, as a globe surrounded by a serpent, whose tail

* Lenormant's *Ancient History of the East*, vol. i. section vii.

is twisted tightly against the solar disk. The serpent decorated the monarch's crown (fig. 89) and fringed the extremities of his

Fig. 90. Royal girdle fringed with jewelled uræi. From figure of K. Seti Menepthah I. (Arundale.)

girdle (fig. 90). In another instance a sphinx, emblem of regal power, under the title, "Lord of the Horizon" (fig. 91), is represented as supported by, or standing between, two procumbent

Fig. 91. Top of an Egyptian standard Sphinx and uræi, implying heavenly victory. (Leemans.)

uræi.* Sometimes, as on the Soane sarcophagus (one of the most wonderful of all Egyptian sarcophagi, originally executed

Fig. 92. The beetle of Chefer Ra, in the Solar orb, surrounded by the serpent Ranno. Possibly the Egyptian original, as far as the Mythos was concerned, of the Orphic figure, No. 28. (Sar. Oimen.)

about the time of Moses, for Oimenepthah or Seti Menepthah I.), the serpent of eternity environs (fig. 92) the disk of the

* See *Musée de Leide*, Part I., plate 21.

sun with seven involutions,* and the circle is completed by the tail of the reptile being placed in its mouth, as in the Greek

Fig. 93. Double snake-headed deity. (Sar. Oimen.)

interpretation.† In the Museum specimen, however, the Coluber, and not the Naja or Cobra, is the species of snake

Fig. 94. Single snake-headed deity wearing the crown of Lower Egypt. (Sar. Oimen.)

adopted. Again on the same work of art is a long vignette representing a number of deities, many of these again being

Fig. 95. Quadruple snake-headed deity holding forth a knife to slay the Apophis. (Sar. Oimen.)

---

* A similar representation at the foot of the sarcophagus of Naskatu, at the British Museum, gives nineteen involutions to the same symbolic serpent.

† See Bonomi's *Sarcophagus of Oimenepthah I.*, plate 5.

snake-headed (fig.93), with ropes and slings (figs.94,95,96,97),

Fig. 96. Single snake-headed deity bringing a rope to bind the Apophis. (Sar. Oimen.)

Fig. 97. The deities binding Apophis from above. (Sar. Oimen.)

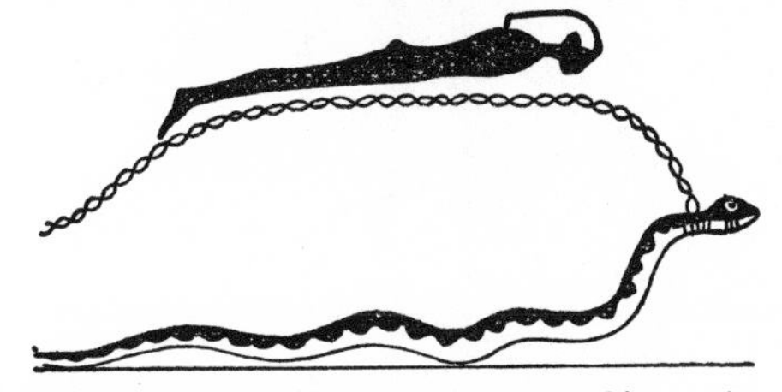

Fig. 98. Another vignette representing the same subject. (Sar. Oimen.)

snaring the Apophis* (fig. 98). Another vignette shows the

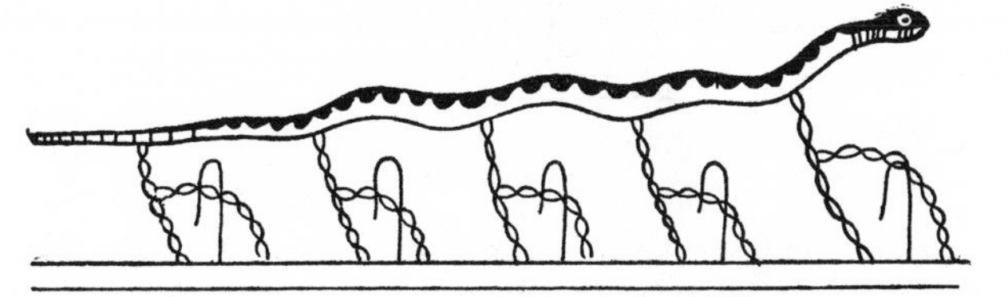

Fig. 99. Apophis bound below with chains and bronze staples. (Sar. Oimen.)

---

* See Bonomi's *Sarcophagus of Oimenepthah I.*, plate 12.

hand of the Eternal holding the enchained monster; another, Apophis chained to the ground by four chains, symbolizing the four races of mankind, fighting against the evil one (fig. 99);* another, Apophis writhing in agony between the assembled gods, who have transfixed him with many knives; another,† Apophis in the mystic lake folded in twenty-eight convolutions; and lastly,‡ Apophis brought

Fig. 100. The serpent "Fire-face" devouring the wicked; the avenging deities are standing upon his folds to restrain his violence within due bounds. (Sar. Oimen.)

prisoner to Horus Ra and slain by that merciful divinity.§ These, as the Ritual has shown, all belong directly to the myth

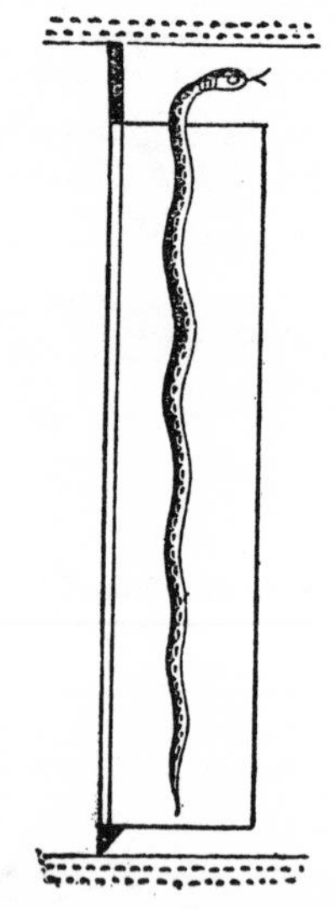

Fig. 101. One of the twelve serpent warders of the twelve doors of Hades. (Sar. Oimen.)

of Apophis; but on the same alabaster sarcophagus is engraven another subject, viz. a troop of wicked men with their hands and

---

* See Bonomi's *Sarcophagus of Oimenepthah I.*, plate 9.
† *Ib.*, plate 15. ‡ *Ib.*, plate 7. § *Ib.*, plate 11.

bows fastened behind them, led by a guardian demon to the presence of a monstrous apophic reptile, called "Fire-face" (a common Ophite epithet), who breathes flames upon them from his open jaws, and consumes the wicked by the breath of his mouth* (fig. 100†). On other parts of the sarcophagus are further shown the gates of Hades (fig. 101), with the mystical

Fig. 102. Winged asp, from the same sarcophagus.‡

serpent warders (fig. 102), the paradise of cypress-trees, guarded by fiery uræi.§ Crocodiles, whose tails end in serpentine forms, Winged serpents, the emblems of the deities Ranno and Maut.

Fig. 103. Four mystic figures treading on a *male* serpent with the crown of Lower Egypt. The serpent's name is Apte. (Sar. Oimen.)

Serpents walking upon human legs (figs. 103, 104), the usual figure of the god Chnuphis, soul of the world. Serpents with human

---

* See Bonomi's *Sarcophagus of Oimenepthah I.*, plate 14.

† "O ye wicked, the flames of Amun-Ra are in thy members, they cannot be extinguished for ever."—Birch, *Magical Papyrus in the British Museum.*

‡ For further details on Winged serpents it is only necessary to quote the search of Demeter for Persephone, in a chariot drawn by Winged serpents.—Creuzer, *Symbolik*, iv. 294.

§ These latter objects it is but fair to state are believed by M. Pierret to be the cresting of the Pylons of the abodes of Amenti.

feminine heads, the representations of the god Atmoo,* the god of darkness, and a basilisk with three faces, the significant

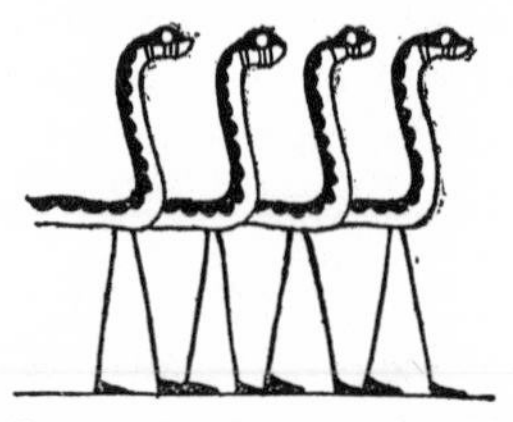

Fig. 104. Four figures similar to preceding. Serpents named Hapu. (Sar. Oimen.)

ideograph of the Egyptian triad of Horus (fig. 106), Isis, and Osiris,—the producing, the producer, and the produced; the

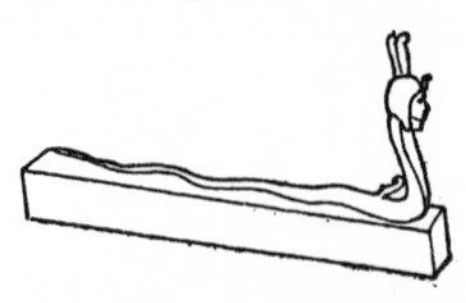

Fig. 105. Votive mummy-case in bronze, containing the mummy of an eel sacred to the god Atum, or Atmoo, the beneficent deity of darkness. (Leemans.)

almost consimilar analogues of the Hindu triad of Elephanta,—Brahma, Vishnu, and Siva.†

Fig. 106. The mystic triune basilisk of Horus, Isis, and Osiris. (Sar. Oimen.)

38. Another sarcophagus illustrating the serpent mythos, is that of Rameses III., the great founder of Medinet Habou, at Cambridge, around the inscribed sides of whose basalt coffin coils an enormous snake; the extremities of the reptile are conjoined, and the figure was probably intended to represent the eternal life of the King protected by the "snake

---

* Sometimes significantly enough represented by an eel, as in the votive eel in the British Museum, case No. 38. (Fig. 105.)

† See Bonomi's *Sarcophagus of Oimenepthah I.*, plate 11.

whose name is millions of years—millions of days encompass him."

39. An undescribed wooden mummy-case lately sold at the Palais Royal,* Regent Street, bore a similar uncommon delineation. In the British Museum are three terra-cotta groups, very roughly executed, of a mother and child (fig. 107) lying upon a

Fig. 107. Funereal tablet, mother and child, protected by the deity Chnuphis. (British Museum.)

couch with a snake, in this instance not the Coluber, but the Asp, encircling them; probably a flattering statuette, implying that the mother and child of the owner should, like Isis and Horus, enjoy the eternal years of divinity.

40. Thus allusion to Horus recalls a circumstance which must not lightly be passed over.† All serpents, even though divine, were not harmless upon this terrene sphere, and as Horus was the great incarnate son of Osiris, whose mission was to overcome evil and to destroy the Apophis, so that divinity became naturally associated with the office of "stopper of all snakes." Hence arose the custom of inscribing votive cippi to that deity, representing him as a youthful and beautiful being, standing upon the heads of two crocodiles, and holding snakes and scorpions in his hands. Above him is always the horrible head of Baal, or Set-Typhon, and the various attributes of life, dominion, power, goodness, &c., with mystic valedictory inscriptions grouped around him. A very fine specimen in wood, and others smaller in stone, are in the British

* By Messrs. Thurgood and Giles, July, 1871. The sarcophagus was of sycamore-wood, and probably dated from the nineteenth dynasty.

† *See* Navielle, *Texte de la Mythe d'Horus*, for fuller details.

Museum ; another as fine in hard wood was formerly in the Hay collection, and has lately gone to Boston, in the United States. A variety of these cippi, at that time supposed by Denon, Wilkinson, and others to be astronomical, are engraved in the "Mémoires" accompanying the *Description de l'Egypt* (fig. 108); and the discoveries of later Egyptologists have

Fig. 108. Talismanic shrine of Horus, the stopper of snakes. On one side stands the staff and quadrangular feathers of the deity Atum, the god of darkness, and on the other the papyrus, staff, and hawk of Horus-Ra. In the centre stands Horus himself, treading upon the heads of two crocodiles, emblems of typhonic power, and in either hand he holds snakes and savage beasts, as restraining their violence. Above him is the head of Set or Baal, whose superhuman power Horus is supposed to have assumed. The usual long lock of hair (accidentally reversed by the artist) hangs over the left shoulder of the deity. (Denon, *Description de l'Egypte.*)

proven, beyond all doubt, from the hieroglyphics themselves, that these objects were universally adopted in ancient Egypt as preservatives against the attacks of all venomous or dan-

Fig. 109. Porcelain amulet (exact size). The snake Nuhab making an offering of wine to the gods.

gerous reptiles by the benevolent protection of Horus, and were even by the Gnostic Christians dedicated to Jehovah as the

God ΙΑΩ.* Sometimes miniature copies of these cippi were manufactured in blue porcelain, and were hung as amulets around the necks of children, as was also a less common figure

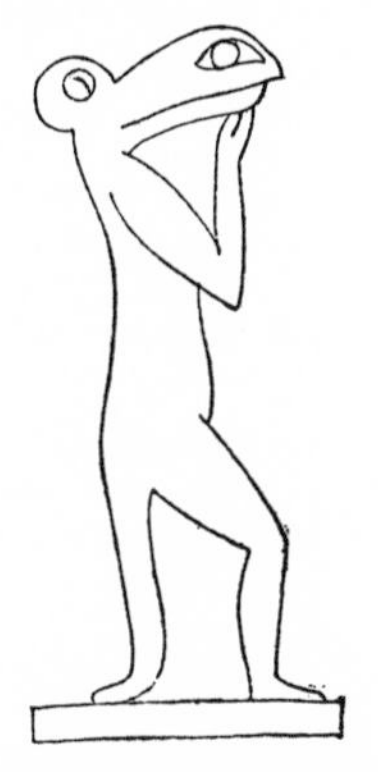

Fig. 110. Porcelain amulet (exact size). Horus the snake-headed. (Hay collection.)

of the god Horus (fig. 109) wearing a serpent's head (fig. 110),† and the talismanic figures of the serpent of Ranno (fig. 111).

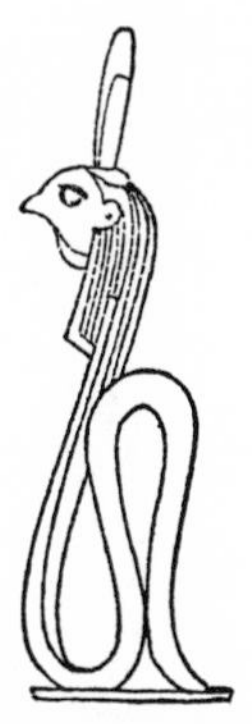

Fig. 111. Amulet (exact size). Horus, as a hawk-headed uræus, wearing the solar disk.

In fact there was, the papyrus only excepted, scarcely any object so frequently used, or represented, either as an emblem of good or evil, as the snake, in its three great varieties,

---

* Montfaucon, tom. ii. planche 370.

† Horus being also mystically identified with the Good Serpent Agathademon.—Wilkinson, v. 398.

or rather genera, of Coluber, Naja, and Asp (fig. 6, etc.). The ancient writers gravely asserted that the sand of the

Fig. 112. Nahab, or Nahab-ka, as in fig. 109.

Theban desert spontaneously generated these dangerous reptiles;* and it would seem as if the whole of the Theban mythology were buried in the cockatrice den, or written upon the skin of a snake.

41. A peculiar malignity, according to the Egyptians, attached itself to a serpent's bite, for not only was it fatal to the living, but the dead themselves became obnoxious to its influence. The pure spirit of the Eternal could not inhabit a body

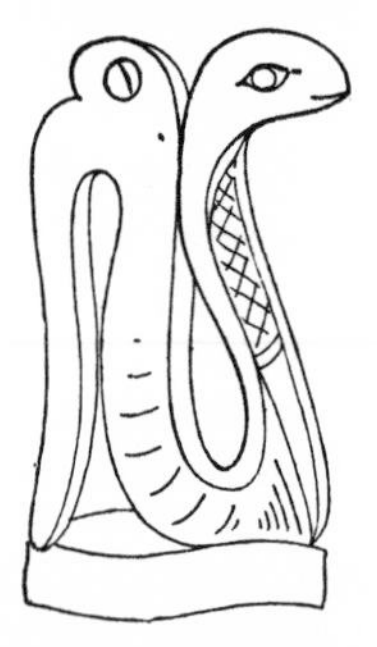

Fig. 113. Steatite amulet (exact size). The goddess Mersokar. (Hay collection.)

infected with the venom of a snake or scorpion.† Hence the mummies of the deceased were protected from ophite injury by

* Diodorus Siculus, lib. i. cap. i.
† *Ritual*, caps. xxxv. and xli.

Fig. 114. Porcelain amulet (exact size). The goddess Ranno. (Hay collection.)

charms, talismans, and incantations (figs. 113, 114). Some of these, of the Greco-Egyptian or Ptolemaic period, have been

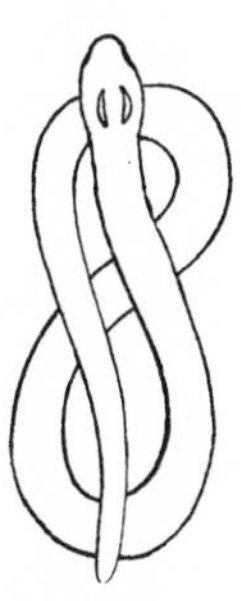

Fig. 115. Wooden amulet for domestic use. Same deity. (Leemans.)

preserved to the present time (fig. 115). The highly symbolical nature of the figures depicted, and mythical character of the words employed, render them exceedingly difficult of interpretation; not to mention the circumstance that in many instances the papyri and tablets have been wilfully defaced, or broken asunder by later sectaries. One of them, engraved by Sharpe, in the *Egyptian Inscriptions*,* has been in part translated by M. Chabas,† and appears to contain, in the first section, a series of directions or rubrics to the mourners or embalmers. After these follows the charm itself, being an adjuration against the serpent's enemies, both in this earth and Amenti, addressed to Horus, the protector of the dead.

"O sheep, son of a sheep, lamb, son of a sheep, who suckest the milk of thy mother the sheep, do not let the defunct be bitten by any serpent, male or female, by any scorpion or any reptile; do not let any one of them possess [have the mastery] over his limbs. Do not let him be penetrated [or possessed] by any male or female dead; may no shade of any spirit haunt him, may the mouth of the serpent Ham-ha-hu-f have no power over him." (Figs. 116, 117.)

* *Egyptian Inscriptions*, fol. 1837, plates 9–12.
† *Bulletin Archéologique*, p. 44, Juin, 1855.

Here the allusions, both to the serpent enemies of the soul and the possibility of the body of one man being interpene-

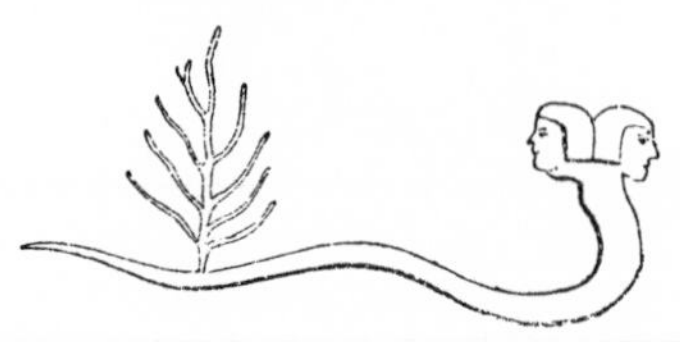

Fig. 116. The serpent germinating. A pictorial representation of a phrase used in the Magical Papyri. (See Birch, "Sur un Papyrus Magique," *Revue Archéologique.*)

trated by the soul of another, and that an evil one,—the doctrine of the Pistis Sophia of the Gnostics, are theologically exceedingly valuable.

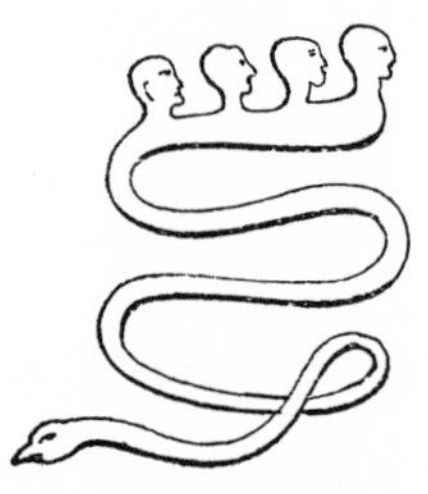

Fig. 117. The four-headed uræus. Another of the ideographic snakes drawn in the Magical Papyri.

Fig. 118. Bronze coin of the Emperor Hadrian, struck at Alexandria, showing the two opposing serpents of good and evil. (Sharpe.)

Fig. 119. A similar coin. The deity Jupiter Serapis, as the serpent of evil, carrying a basket upon his head. (Sharpe.)

42. It were at this stage of the inquiry too long and too modern a subject to trace the myth of the serpent, as the antago

Fig. 120. The serpent of evil riding on a horse, emblematic of the terrible rapidity of its progress. From a Gnostic coin. (Sharpe.)

nistic powers of good and evil,* through the subtleties of the Gnostic commentators (figs. 121, 122, 123, 124), and the heresy

Fig. 121. The mystic serpent of the Gnostics, standing upon a wheel and holding a club. From a gem. (Montfaucon.) Compare the Chuktra and serpent of Buddist mythology.†

Fig. 122. The serpent Chnuphis, spelled Chmoymem, with the seven-rayed crown, emblematic of the seven mystic potentialities. On one side is his name, on the other an emblem of the Gnostic trinity, and beneath him the petition Abraxas, *i.e.*, "hurt me not." (?) (Montfaucon.)

---

* Among the magical emblems of the Egyptians was an uræus on a wheel. The creature is called Akhi Sesef, "the Turner of Destruction," "the Mistress of the Burning Wheel, who lives off [by devouring] impurity."—Birch, *Magic Papyrus.*

† On the Egyptian coins of Hadrian, for example, where the two serpents and the heads respectively of Isis and Serapis represent the antagonistic powers, *see* Sharpe, *History of Egypt*, vol. ii. chap. 15. (Figs. 118, 119, 120.)

Fig. 123. A similar gem. Around the leonine head of the serpent are the uncial Greek characters composing his name.*

Fig. 124. Another similar gem, very late Roman. The inscription probably means "Abraxas, name of God,"—ABRESSES, NUMEN (for nomen) DAEI (for dei), miswritten by the ignorance of the Alexandrian seal-engraver. (Montfaucon.)

Fig. 125. Chnuphis walking crowned with seven stars (a form afterwards much used by the Gnostics. See fig. 97). (Denon.)

---

* "In the beginning, earth and water, to mud condensing, united. Afterwards a third principle was born, a serpent with the heads of a bull and a lion, and in the midst the face of a god; it had wings on its shoulders, and was called Χρόνος αγήρατος."—*Teste* Hellanicus, quoted in Creuzer's *Symbolik*, pp. 81–4. See also King, C. W., *The Gnostics and their Remains*, plates v. and vii.

of Basilius into the Christian religion (fig. 125). It was as if the giant Apophis, of Egypt, in dying under the spear of Alexandrian Christianity, infected its destroyer with its envenomed breath, and poisoned whom it could not over-

Fig. 126. A very curious Greco-Egyptian Gnostic seal (considerably enlarged). Christ with the attributes of Horus, treading upon the crocodile of evil, and holding the sacred symbol of his name, a fish, ιχθυς, i.e. Ιησους Χριστος Θεου Υιος Σωτηρ (Jesus Christ, the Son of God, the Saviour). This gem is peculiarly valuable, as showing how easily the Alexandrian Christians introduced their ancient emblems and their corresponding theories into the rising Christianity of Egypt. (From the collection in the British Museum.)

power* (fig. 126). The subject is a wide, a grave, and a sacred one, and if studied at all must be reverently and unbiassedly studied. Close we the story of Egyptian Ophiolatry here, and in as few words as may be compatible with the lateness of the hour, and the extent of the materials, summarize the results of this imperfect examination.

43. I. That in the Egyptian mythology, the oldest which, apart from the Bible, has been handed down to us, and is clearly

---

(Note on some of the preceding names of serpents.)

* Abraxas אוֹב רוּח fallen spirit (?) Ab-rahak. From Ezekiel i. 15-16. Cabbala-Sohar gives אוֹפן Ophan (wheel) an order of Angels, as כְּרוּב Krub (cherub). שָׂטָן (Satan) from שׂוּט (shoot) wandering, Job i. 7 ; ii. 2. אַף אַף Aph-aph,—anger, wrath (of God). אֲנַף (Anaph), foaming with rage אַף Nose, inflated nostrils wing, Kanaph כָּנָף ?—S. M. Drach.

traceable for three thousand years B.C.,* there are preserved, along with others, though in a corrupted and exaggerated form, many of the great doctrines of revealed religion.

II. That, prominent above other myths in that religious system, was the belief in a monstrous *personal* evil being,† typically represented as a serpent, and whose office was to accuse the righteous, oppose the Supreme Deity, and devour the wicked.

III. That, co-existently in the order of time, there arose a dualistic principle of good, likewise represented, for scarcely intelligible reasons, by an entirely different serpent, and that between these two a constant spiritual warfare was maintained.‡

IV. That, in the abstract, both good and evil were directly produced by *one* Supreme Being, who also co-operated with the righteous in their endeavours after holiness.

V. That the doctrine of the Metempsychosis, and the dogmas of Purgatory, vicarious propitiation, a tangible Hades, Heaven and Hell, were also a part of the Egyptian Cultus.

VI. That negative and positive holiness, rewards and punishments, and conformity to the divine nature, were doctrines of the same theology.

VII. That the supreme delight of the justified consisted in *conscious* hypostatic union with the Eternal Being,§ which was attainable only after much purgation, and long-continued effort.

VIII. That the final punishment of the wicked consisted in utter annihilation, after a period of frightful torture in a fiery hell.

IX. That the contest between good and evil would be at last terminated by the incarnation of Deity overcoming the great serpent, and utterly destroying him.‖

X. That besides all this, the serpent myths originated other symbolisms indirectly connected with the preceding dogmas, and that these, not being revealed by the priests to the general body of the people, were by them misunderstood.

---

* Lenormant, Bunsen, and Wilkinson.

† Satan שָׂטָן Sheitan, the hinderer, or from *shoot* שׁוּט = שְׁט the wanderer (Job i. 7, and ii. 2).

‡ See also Plutarch, *De Iside;* and Bunsen, *Egypt's Place in Universal History*, vol. i. book i., for a fuller account of the Osiri-Typhonic myth.

§ Differing herein essentially from the Nirwana or repose of Buddhism.

‖ See also for a brief popular résumé of the principal of these doctrines, Keary, *Early Egyptian History*, pp. 364–409.

. XI. That the principal corruptions of primitive Christianity arose from the Platonists and Gnostics of the Greco-Egyptian capital Alexandria,* in the same manner as their own ancient religion was originally derived from a purer source, *now only to be found in the Bible.*

XII. That the study of Egyptian mythology will throw more light upon the restrictive customs of the Jews,† the allusions of the prophets, and the early history of the Christian church, than that of any other country.

Thus then for a time we roll back the papyrus on which is inscribed the story of the serpent Apophis, ask we, Why the Father of Mankind has permitted these records to contain, amid so many errors, much to testify of prophetic and spiritual truth? Seek then the answer in the words of the Apostle of the Gentiles,‡ "God left not himself without witness in the world," so that even by the light of nature, "all the world might become guilty before Him," and might in the fulness of time be saved by His Son who is God over all, the victor over the great dragon, "that old serpent," for ever—and evermore.

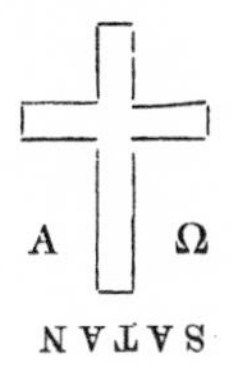

* Sharpe, *Egyptian Mythology and Egyptian Christianity.*

† See particularly Chabas, F., "Hebræo-Egyptiaca," *Trans. Soc. Bib. Archæology,* vol. i.; and Laüth, *Moses der Ebraeer,* 1868, which, although wrong in its conclusions, throws much light on early Jewish history.

‡ Acts xiv. 17.

APPENDIX.

It may interest Philologists to see all the names and significant epithets of the various serpents or serpent-formed Deities of Egypt in one list :—

Names of Apophis.

Apap, Apepi, Apophis, Apopth, App, Baba, Bebon, Bth, Chf, Chof, Ho, Hof, Sba, Sutekh.

Names of the Soul of the World.

Bai, Bait, Bat, Knum, Chnouphis, Chnumis.

Names of other Serpents.

Fenti, Gatfi, Ham, Har, Hu-ef, Mersokar, 'Mhn, Nfi, Nu, Ru, Ruhak, Tetbi, Urtuk, Urhapt ? †

The vowels being in many cases wanting, the true etymology of these names cannot now be recovered.

English Translations of Epithets applied in the Ritual of the Dead to the various Serpents referred to.

Adversary (Bunsen).
Beast (Bunsen).
Breaker of the Wicked.
* Brass of Earth.
* Circling (Sar. Oimen.—epithet, 1st doorkeeper).
Clasper (Bunsen).
Consumer (Bunsen).
Destroyer (Bunsen).
* Devourer (Sar. Oimen., Apophis).
Enemy (Bunsen).

---

† *All* the feminine deities were, as before stated, either represented or were venerated under the form of uræi.—Birch.

Erector (Bunsen).
Fire-face (cap. 145—2nd hall).
* Fire in his Eye (Sar. Oimen.—8th doorkeeper).
Flame-face (cap. 145—5th hall).
Giant (Bunsen).
Great Clasper.
* Horn of the Earth (Sar. Oimen.—3rd doorkeeper of Amenti).
* Spark-face (Sar. Oimen.—7th doorkeeper of Amenti).
* Sparkling Face (Sar. Oimen.—7th doorkeeper of Amenti).
Spitter of Fire.
Stopper of the Rejected (cap. 145—7th hall).
Stone Head (cap. 145—6th hall).
The Great Destroyer.
* The Living (Sar. Oimen.).
The wicked, *Sba* (Bunsen).

For the names of the Snakes distinguished by an asterisk the author is indebted to the courtesy of the distinguished hieroglyphist Dr. S. Birch.

The CHAIRMAN.—I am sure that we all desire to return a cordial vote of thanks to Mr. Cooper for his able and interesting paper. (Cheers.)

Rev. J. JAMES.—I should like to ask Mr. Cooper one question: In what character is this Ritual of the Dead written—in hieroglyphic, hieratic or demotic?

Mr. COOPER.—It is generally found in the hieroglyphic and hieratic characters. In the oldest papyri the writing is almost purely ideographic. The demotic script is very similar to the hieratic, but far less intelligible; having more resemblance to an exceedingly bad school-boy's hand of the present time.

Mr. JAMES.—Do you mean that there are three characters of the same things—sometimes the hieroglyphic, sometimes the hieratic, and sometimes the demotic?

Mr. COOPER.—Yes; three styles of writing the same language prevailed throughout Egypt for four thousand years. The language was written in hieroglyphic and hieratic, or demotic, side by side, just as you might print the Prayer-book in black-letter and in italic or any other character.

Mr. JAMES.—Are there not several manuscripts of this liturgy?

Mr. COOPER.—M. Le Page Renouf has enumerated and collated 272. Among them are, the copy of Leyden, which contains, I think, a hundred perfect chapters, and the copy of Turin, which contains a hundred and fifty chapters. But there are so many copies in existence that what is wanting in one is supplied in another, and in that way we get altogether the one hundred and sixty-six chapters of which the book is composed.

Rev. J. H. TITCOMB.—I should like to draw attention to what I may call a little bit of comparative mythology. We have been much interested to-night in the serpent myths of Egypt. Some time since I read an account of the Scandinavian mythology, and almost the identical picture is there presented which we find in the 23rd section of this paper. The Scandinavian, like the Egyptian mythology, represented a lake with the evil spirit under the form of a serpent, and the gods in conflict with that serpent. Thor is in conflict with the serpent Midgar on a lake ; the serpent rises and nearly overturns the boat in which he is. The circumstance is interesting as showing how, apart from Egypt, in remote periods of time and in different portions of the globe, we have a reproduction of the same myth. It is an extraordinary piece of evidence of the unity of the human race, and of the common origin of these myths as drawn from one centre—the Word of God. With reference to the same subject of comparative mythology and serpent myths, it may be interesting to you for me to read an extract from a work by Squier, entitled *Serpent Symbol in America*. He gives a remarkable account of one of the traditions of the Lenappi Indians, and describes a great conflict between Manabozho, the presiding genius of the tribe, and the Spirit of Evil represented as a large serpent. The words are as follows :—

"One day, returning home from a long journey, Manabozho, the Great Teacher of the Alonquins, missed his cousin who lived with him. He called his name, but received no answer. He looked around on the sand for the track of his feet, and there for the first time discovered the trail of the great serpent, Meshekenabek, the Spirit of Evil. Then he knew that his cousin had been seized by his great enemy. He armed himself and followed on his track ; passed the great river ; crossed over mountains to the shores of the deep lake where he dwelt. The bottom of the lake was filled with evil spirits, his attendants and companions. In the centre of them he saw Meshekenabek himself, coiling his volumes around his hapless cousin. His head was red as with blood, and his eyes glowed like fire. Manabozho looked on this and vowed vengeance. He directed the clouds to disappear from the heavens, the winds to be still, and the air to become stagnant over the lake, and bade the sun to shine on it fiercely, in order that his enemy might be drawn forth from the cool shadows of the trees. By-and-by the water became troubled, and bubbles rose to the surface, for the rays of the sun penetrated to the horrible brood within its depths. The commotion increased, and the hot waves dashed wildly against the rocks on its shore. Soon Meshekenabek, the great serpent, emerged slowly to the surface and moved towards the shore. Manabozho, who had transformed himself into the stump of a tree, then silently drew an arrow from his quiver and aimed at the heart of his enemy. The howl of the monster shook the mountains, for he was mortally wounded."

This is an instance gained in another and still more distant part of the world, among the rude tribes of North America, where the serpent myth crops up in a way that one would least expect, and in a manner analogous to that of Egypt. Here is a copy of a picture of the Judgment-hall of Osiris from the very papyrus of which Mr. Cooper has been speaking—that at Turin ; but instead of explaining it myself, I shall ask him to do so for you.

Mr. Cooper. — This picture, which Mr. Titcomb has so kindly brought with him, is copied from a well-known vignette in the Ritual of the Dead, but it differs from some that I have seen. Generally speaking, these illustrations have an altar with the four gods of the dead upon it, because the deceased entreats those four gods to intercede for him; but this papyrus is better and more accurate. You have not the four gods of the dead here, but in their place is Horus, the son of God himself, who intercedes standing in a reverential attitude with his hands put together, praying that hs father Orisis may save the deceased, pardon, and admit him to the abodes of the blessed. Horus stands between the deceased and hell, here represented as a temple filled with fire, and over hell sits the monster Typho, "the devourer of the souls of the unjustified"; between hell and the judge is an altar containing fruit and flowers, supposed to have been offered by the deceased, when alive, to Horus, who now offers *his* mediation for the deceased. By the steelyard is represented a monkey, the emblem of justice, because all his extremities are hands, and all are equal. In one scale is the goddess of Truth, and in the other is a little vase containing the heart of the deceased. If it is equal in weight, the deceased is acquitted; if it is not, he is condemned. The deceased stands between the goddesses Isis and Nepthys, and he bows before the judge, with one hand on his breast, while the other shrouds his face, for it is necessary, in standing before a god, or in praying to the Serpent, to put the hand before the face. The figure of Thoth is seen

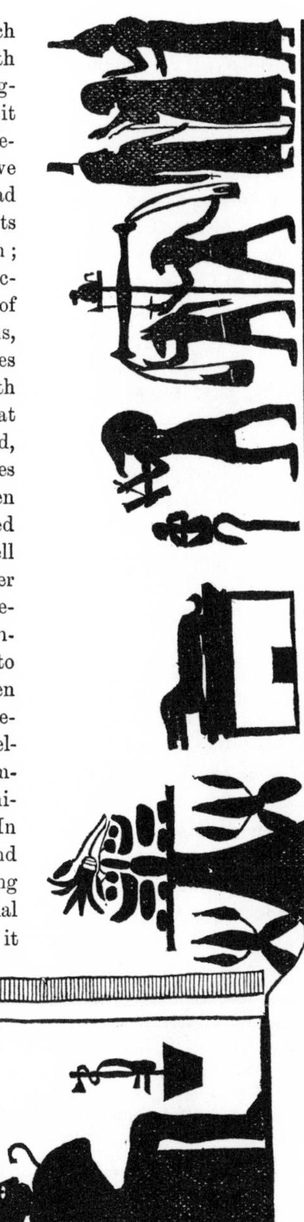

The Judgment Hall of Osiris.

writing down the good deeds of the deceased, and the result of his acquittal or condemnation. I am much obliged to Mr. Titcomb for bringing this picture.

Mr. I. T. PRICHARD.—I cannot throw much light upon the subject, but having been in India, may be able to give a little evidence from modern times in reference to the very peculiar veneration that the natives of India have for serpents, even the most venomous. The kind of cobra that Mr. Cooper has mentioned is very common in India, and even the most venomous serpents that we find occasionally in the gardens or in the houses it is impossible to get any of the natives of the lower classes to touch. They will not kill them, but are desperately afraid of them, because a bite is generally death, though with proper measures life can be saved. I have often inquired the reason, but they never give any—they merely say it is against their religion. They have some religious objection against injuring these creatures, and it would certainly seem as if some kind of tradition had been handed down from early times that these reptiles had a sort of sanctity about them, and hence the people are afraid of touching them, even in self-defence. I speak from the experience of very recent years.

Mr. COOPER.—The common Egyptians likewise never touched the serpent: they had too much reverence for it. They always carried it in an ark borne by four priests, and only occasionally exhibited it to the vulgar eye.

Rev. S. WAINWRIGHT, D.D.—I presume that paragraph 4, section 43, is to be regarded as only giving the result of Mr. Cooper's inquiries in Egyptian Mythology apart from the Bible, because it refers to a point which neither he nor we recognize as belonging to Revealed Religion—I allude to the words, "In the abstract, both good and evil were directly produced by *one* Supreme Being." Another point I wish to mention is that to which Mr. Titcomb referred—the Scandinavian Mythology, to show that there too, there was an account of a boat on a lake—it occurred to me to suggest that perhaps that idea of the boat which we find existing in lands so far remote, may be a sort of floating tradition of the ark.

Mr. COOPER.—In common with all the Hamitic races, there is no flood tradition in Egypt.*

---

* There is no quarter of the globe where modern discovery can play a more important part than in Africa, as comparatively little is known about it. In regard to Mr. Cooper's statement, I find a well-known modern writer on geology says,—"There seems to exist no such definite outline of the Egyptian tradition referred to by Josephus as that preserved of the Chaldean one. Even in Egypt, however, the recollection of the Deluge seems to have survived, though it lay entangled amid what seem to be symbolized memories of unusual floodings of the river Nile." The "Noah of Egypt," says Professor Hitchcock, "appears to have been Osiris, and it is a curious fact that he embarked on the 17th day of the month Athyr, the very day, most probably, when Noah entered the ark." I may add that, as regards the Chaldean account of the flood, Mr. G. Smith has recently found the fragments of an Assyrian tablet from Nineveh, in the British Museum; the inscription,

Dr. Wainwright.—Well, there are two more points on which I should be glad to have information. We know that certain classes of serpents are poisonous, and I should like to know if such are found in a fossil state; also, if the Egyptians always represented serpents as cumbent.

Mr. Cooper.—The deductions given towards the close of my paper are deductions from the mythology of Egypt, and my own faith winds up the last paragraph, which I believe to be orthodox. As to fossil serpents being venomous or non-venomous I do not know how that may be borne out; I believe that they were not venomous. The Serpent of Good is always represented by the Egyptians as upright, and the Serpent of Evil as crawling, and that is generally the only distinction which they make.

Rev. G. Henslow.—Fossil serpents are very rare; geologists know very little about them; but in the Eocene clay snakes have been found, which Professor Owen considers as probably frequenting water.

Mr. Cooper.—The water-snake is never represented in Egypt.

Mr. Henslow.—There is a snake-like form of animal among the Assyrian monuments.

Mr. Cooper.—It is an emblem of Hea, the Assyrian water deity. With respect to the eel, the Egyptians knew of it, but they dedicated it to the God of Darkness. As to the boat, there is quite evidence enough about the character of the mystic bark of the sun—the Divine Baris—without troubling ourselves about it in this case. The Nile was the great highway of the Egyptians, and it is natural enough to represent the sun as travelling by water—the only road he could travel by; more especially as they believed, with the early Pelasgians mentioned by Herodotus, that the world was entirely surrounded by an impassable ocean in which the deities sailed and beyond which they resided, a theory which has an Indian analogue in the cosmos of the Buddhists, and, if I mistake not, is also preserved in the Eddas of the Scandinavian nations. If they had travelled as the Assyrians did, by land, they would have represented the sun as walking, or have put him, as other nations did, on the backs of horses—as for instance the Greeks, who put Phaëton in his *quadriga*.

Rev. C. A. Row.—From the book called "The Ritual of the Dead," do you conclude that the Egyptian theology was of an exclusively pantheistic character? I want to know whether the idea of deity involved freedom of will, or fate—whether it conceived of him, or not, as a living person? Also,

---

which is in Semitic Babylonian, was copied B.C. 660 from a Chaldean document at Erech, at least as old as the 17th century B.C., and contains many of the events of the flood, but given in a legendary style, and with certain minor differences, which show that it embodies a distinct and independent tradition belonging to distinct peoples. Mr. G. Smith, when reading a paper on this inscription before the Society of Biblical Archæology, in November, 1872, remarked on the value of the histories that are stored in the mounds and ruined cities now buried in the plains of Chaldea, once the cradle of civilization.—[Ed.]

what are the ideas of the soul; whether immortality was regarded as more or less involving a personal existence ?

Mr. COOPER.—First of all, the Supreme Deity of the Egyptians was Ammon-Ra, the spiritual author of all existence, physical, moral, and everything else. But that was too abstract an idea for the people to grasp, especially those of Lower Egypt. Therefore the priests typified all the attributes of deity, and thus came near to the Persian system; but for all this they never lost sight of one Supreme Being, while the people invariably did, and that is the great distinction between them. As would naturally follow from such a system, they were not distinct about their deities; one man would worship a god under the form of Sate, while another would worship the same god under the name of Isis, and another under that of Nepthys. They had triads of gods,—a male, female, and a child; but they were not all the same triads, though all were more or less symbolized or crowned by serpents. All the goddesses were serpents; there is no evidence to suppose that the Supreme Being was ever lost sight of by those who knew the esoteric meaning of the Egyptian faith. As to the soul, it was a distinct personality, separate from the body, emanating from the Supreme Being; it had to answer for its misdoings, and if, at the death of the body, it was not good enough, it had to come back to earth to be purged. But if it were good, it would go in a condition of extreme happiness into the presence of God, and assume the character of one or other of the inferior divinities for an *æon;* but then it would come back to earth, lose all its consciousness of existence, and become the soul of somebody else. But it could not inhabit any other body without the permission of the Supreme Being, and if it found its original body all crumbled to pieces, or if another spirit had by some evil means possessed it, the unhappy soul would have to float about like the disembodied ghosts in Virgil. For this reason people were very anxious for the preservation of their bodies after death. But it was believed that in some rare instances, where the original body was completely destroyed, the Supreme Being gave the soul permission to inhabit some other body. In the time of the Ptolemies it was thought to be possible that the soul and body might mistake each other at the resurrection to life, and hence arises much of the beautiful Platonic myths of Eros and Psyche. The resurrection of all men was not held by them as by us: they believed that all men would be judged, but not all at the same time.

Mr. ROW.—How far is the pantheon of Egypt allied to the pantheon of India ?

Mr. COOPER.—At present nobody can definitely tell us that. We have some material as to the ancient religion of hither India in the pre-Bhuddist period, and there is a great similarity between that and the Egyptian, but we cannot dogmatize on the subject. The Egyptian mythology was perfect at least 4,000 years before Christ, and all we can say is that everything in the Indian mythology meets its analogue in the Egyptian mythology. When the Semitic people came across with Rameses from India and conquered the aboriginal races, they introduced much of their own cultus, but they also adopted Egyptian forms, the result being a very great change indeed ; and it is possible that the Rameside may have introduced an Indian mythology with them, or, at all events, have explained Turanian myths by Semitic theories.

Mr. Row.—Was the Egyptian theology a personification of the powers of nature ?

Mr. Cooper.—No ; but that the theurgia of a Supreme Being manifested in the powers of nature.

Mr. Row.—But was it not simply a personification of the powers of nature ?

Mr. Cooper.—By no means. [Mr. Cooper here drew upon the black board representations of the head of an ancient Egyptian, and of the head of one of the men of the Rameside period, to show the degeneration in the physiological character of the races. He then proceeded to say :] It was an Indo-Germanic race that conquered Egypt in the time of the Rameses, and made great improvements. All the remains of Egypt, except the pyramids and one or two imperfect tombs, belong to that race. There was also another conquering race of a different or Arabian type, whose influence again modified the Egyptian cultus, but it has left very few evidences. They seem to have possessed no literature, and no evidence of their sway remained except the extreme hatred that every Egyptian bore to the shepherd or Hykshos rulers.

Rev. T. M. Gorman.—I should like to ask one question which seems to have an important bearing on the *rationale* of this curious and difficult subject. In the paper just read reference has been made to the idea of a spiritual Supreme Being as known to the most ancient Egyptians. Can Egyptologers throw any light on the *origin* of this idea ? It would be a point of great interest to show that the idea was derived, not from the fancy, or even the reason of this originally grave and thoughtful people, but from the primeval Revelation. It appears to me that the real and lasting value of researches such as these depends materially upon the solution of questions like that here proposed. If carefully and patiently worked out, considerable light might be thrown on the true character and purport of Egyptian symbolism, a subject full of interest for the Christian student of ancient lore. As an illustration of what is meant, may be mentioned the adoption of the serpent, by the Egyptians, for an emblem of evil, as opening up one of the most difficult questions in theology. The study of this and kindred subjects brings before us a fact which deserves our best consideration in these days ; namely, the power and depth of the thinking faculty as evinced by the nations of the Old World in the records that have been preserved of their national life. Upwards of twenty centuries ago the Egyptians had fallen away from their pristine enlightenment. Their state is described in the inspired words of the Hebrew prophet :—"The princes of Zoan are fools, the counsel of the wise counsellors of Pharaoh is become brutish." It was not so in the old time. We learn on the same authority that Egypt was once called "the son of the wise, the son of the kings of antiquity." Were it possible to arrive at the primal source of the knowledge possessed by the Egyptians of the Supreme Deity, as a spiritual creator and governor, something perhaps might be done in the way of solving another difficult problem—the separation of what is genuine from what is spurious in Egyptian mythology. It might thus be possible to distinguish, more clearly than has yet been done, the truth—of which the symbol is the expression—from the fable by which, in the lapse of ages, that truth has been overgrown and well-nigh lost to view. By working assiduously in the same direction it might be possible to lessen in some degree the confusion of truth and myth which at present exists in the older Greek and Roman mythology. For here also have been preserved some remnants of a true symbolism. To discover, then, the source of that spiritual idea of the Deity which once prevailed among this ancient and peculiar people, would, it seems to me, impart a new and living interest to researches such as those on which the instructive paper of this evening is based, and place students of Egyptology in a much more advantageous position for estimating the true value of results arrived at in this branch of learning. The acute remark of a well-informed writer on the subject well deserves to be borne in mind in the present connection :—" The Egyptians are not the only people who have converted type into substance, or adopted in a literal sense the metaphorical symbols of faith."

Mr. Cooper.—The book that contains the answer to that question is very abstruse and difficult to understand, because it is written in purely ideographic symbolism. It is the book of the Manifestations, or Liturgy of the Sun, and has been published by M. Chabas. We cannot obtain much from it otherwise than that the abstract sense of Deity is represented by the first of all symbols—fire ; by light, and air, and by everything beautiful. There is a passage that implies that the Deity is holiness also.

Rev. C. Graham.—With regard to the mythology of Greece and Rome, you will find that it illustrates many of the great facts in the Book of Genesis. Of course it does so in a corrupted form ; but nevertheless those facts are illustrated, and I would venture to say that they are derived from Egyptian mythology. In Genesis we are told most distinctly that a serpent induced Eve to eat of the forbidden fruit. Now in the Greek and Roman mythology we have the Garden of the Hesperides, supposed to be just on the borders of Ethiopia. We have a serpent coiled round the tree defending the golden apples, and Atlas surrounding the gardens with mountains in order to prevent the fulfilment of an ancient prophecy that the son of a god would at length destroy the serpent and take off the apples. Another fact recorded in Genesis is, that the seed of the woman was to bruise the head of the serpent. Now in mythology we have that great truth also transmitted. We have, for instance, Hercules destroying the serpent with his club, according to Apollonius ; and according to Ovid and others, we have Apollo destroying the Python with his arrows. These facts, which lie at the foundation of our religion, are distinctly transmitted from classic mythology, and in all probability they passed from Egypt to Greece and Rome. With regard to the word Hesperides itself, many learned men derive it from the Hebrew word *ets peri*—a tree of fruit. The serpent, according to Apollonius, is called Ladon, which learned men derive from *El Adon*, the God of Eden, attributing to the serpent divine power, and making it a god. These matters are important. I do not know whether Mr. Cooper would tell us that the mythology of Greece and Rome was mainly derived from an Egyptian source.

Mr. COOPER.—Oh no, not in your sense. No doubt Egypt is the mother of those mythologies, but she has very bad daughters.

Mr. GRAHAM.—Just so. But in these cases the mythology of Greece and Rome is more distinct and illustrative, even than that of ancient Egypt. The great facts of the Fall and of the Redemption come out most distinctly in the mythology of Greece and Rome.

Mr. COOPER.—Far less so as matters of doctrine, to my belief, than they do in Egypt ; the great distinction between physical and moral evil, and the sense of human responsibility prevailing far more largely in the Egyptian faith than it did either in Hellene or Latin theology. Plato doubted of what God was made, and Pliny doubted if there were a Supreme Deity at all. The great men were philosophical sensualists, and the people unreflecting fetischists.

Mr. J. ALLEN.—You spoke of the Egyptian mythology being perfect 4,000 years before Christ. I suppose you mean according to the chronology of the Egyptians themselves.

Mr. COOPER.—Chronologists differ very much. There are those who, like Sharpe, fix the initial date at about 2,200 before Christ, and others, like Bunsen and Lenormant, who throw it back to 5,000 years ; but those are mere theories until we get more astronomical facts. We have got some atronomical facts however ;—in the reign of Rameses III. eclipses and stellar phenomena are recorded at the temple of Medinet Habou, which, some say, could only have occurred 4,000 or 5,000 years ago. But then a great deal depends upon how far the inscriptions can be chronologically arranged. With regard to the Bible, the Pentateuch is full of Egypt. I think that it was written in the Egyptian alphabet, for a people saturated with the symbolism and the culture of Egypt ; and I consider that the Hebrew characters did not exist at that time, or for centuries afterwards. If this be so, when Moses wrote the early sacred books the writing must have been ideographic or in pictorial hieroglyphic characters; and in all probability he followed out the plan of the Egyptians, conveying partly by symbols, partly by signs, and partly by a mixture of both, the doctrines which were afterwards put into good Hebrew by Ezra and the later priests.* That does not

---

* The *present* Hebrew character was introduced to the Jews from Chaldæa, probably about the time of the Babylonian captivity ; but that is no reason

impugn the truth of the Bible at all; but though, as a book, it may be in some respects comparatively modern, the doctrines of the Bible are coeval with the origin of the human race itself, and could only have been made known by divine revelation. We have proved that book to be absolutely true in matters of history;* and I believe we shall prove it to be absolutely true in matters of theology also; but that must be done by different persons. If you take a circle, and all men travel in direct lines from its circumference, they will all converge in a common centre. That centre in this case is orthodoxy—any divergence from it is only apparent, not real. (Cheers.)

Dr. WAINWRIGHT.—It has been shown by Professor Donald that in the time of Moses Hebrew was already a language, and had attained a certain stage of consolidation; as is shown by the fossilized character of certain of its elements. There are interesting indications of the extreme antiquity of the language, which show that in the time of Moses it had such an antiquity as to possess other previous stages corresponding to the earlier stages of our own language in the time of Chaucer.

Mr. COOPER.—That is a matter of text, and the oldest copy of the Hebrew Bible in England dates from about the eighth century; my authority is Professor Lenormant—indeed, we have no copy of any writing in Greek, Latin, or Hebrew so old as the time of our Lord, but we have Egyptian inscriptions that can be traced up certainly to 2,000 or 3,000 years before Christ. I do not now allude to incised inscriptions.† It is a curious fact that, as far as written testimony goes, we have none earlier than the Christian era, except the Egyptian papyri and the Assyrian magical

---

for assuming that the language had not an archaic character of its own, or that Moses wrote in the ideographic Egyptian. The Moabite stone, 900 B.C., recently discovered (*see* p. 125), is written in pure Hebrew, but in the ancient Phœnician character; in which character, most probably, the Pentateuch itself was written—(J. H. T.) Dr. Espin remarks (*Speakers' Commentary*, vol. ii. p. 11),—"Archaisms, found in the writings of Moses, are not found in the book of Joshua, and there are traces in the latter that the language had somewhat developed itself in the interval."—[ED.]

* There are some remarkable instances of this given in the Transactions of the "Palestine Exploration Fund" for 1872, which are now added to the Institute's Library. [ED.]

† Since this discussion, Mr. Ganneau has mentioned, as regards ancient Hebrew inscriptions, that "up to this time the texts found in Palestine and Jerusalem are few in number and of small importance: amongst them are two Hebrew texts in Phœnician character discovered at Siloam. Two Hebrew cachets in Phœnician characters give the Biblical names of Ananias, Azarias, and Achbor. These four texts belong to the time of the kings of Judah; also several inscriptions in square Hebrew." To these I may add the seal of Haggai (520 B.C.), the authenticity of which is, however, not yet admitted by all, and the Moabite stone. A curious remark is made by Josephus, *Antiq.*, xii. ii. 1; it is that Demetrius Phalerius, library-keeper to Ptolemy Philadelphus (277 B.C.), spoke of the Hebrew as "similar in sound and character to the language proper to the Syrians."—[ED.]

pottery, I see there is a Hebrew scholar present who will perhaps say a few words on the subject.

Mr. S. M. Drach.—Doctors and Rabbis say that every copy, of the Pentateuch especially, is a reproduction with the greatest minuteness of the original one, supposed to have been written by Moses himself. The Rabbis say that the Pentateuch was originally written in characters generally known as Hebrew or Samaritan, but it is generally allowed that Moses wrote the Pentateuch in alphabetical writing, and there is a great distinction between that and hieroglyphic writing. If we were to adopt Mr. Cooper's idea, and only go upon written testimony, we might well doubt that Homer's writings were written by Homer. Although it is the orthodox Jewish belief that the writings of the Old Testament were in the original language of mankind, yet I must dissent from that. There are a good many synonyms and Jewish words which are perhaps derived from an Indo-Germanic root ; so that the Hebrew of the Pentateuch and of the Old Testament generally is something like the English language, which is formed partly of Latin and partly of Anglo-Saxon ; or like the Spanish, which is partly Latin and partly Arabic ; and not a pure language, such as the German. *Vide David Kimchi on Synonyms*, "*Sh'met Nirdafim.*" (12th century.)

The discussion then closed.

INDEX